The
Rascals *from*
Haskell's Gym

by FRANK BONHAM

Cover by Ruth Sanderson

SCHOLASTIC BOOK SERVICES
NEW YORK • TORONTO • LONDON • AUCKLAND • SYDNEY • TOKYO

Acknowledgments

In keeping technical matters straight in the writing of this story, I had the advice and assistance of a number of coaches and gymnasts. I should like to thank the following persons, among others, who helped me:

Coaches: Glen Vaughan, Bonnie Ratzin, Raquel Stubbs, and Tex Womack of the San Diego Downtown Y Gymnastics Club; and Ed and Darla Franz, of the Aztecs Gymnastics Club, also of San Diego.

My special thanks goes to the girls of the San Diego Y gymnastics team, who helped me greatly at workouts and meets.

ISBN 0-590-30231-0

12 11 10 9 8 7 6 5 4 3 2 1   10   9/7 0 1 2 3 4/8

*This book is dedicated to the girls of the
San Diego Downtown Y Gymnastics Club —
with a special award of 10 points to
Diane Murphy!*

Contents

Butterflies and Raskells

Sissy Benedict had not felt so silly in years. She and eleven other girls from the Butterflies Gymnastic Club were lined up on the judging platform before the livestock barn at the Meadowdale Towne Faire, like animals about to be judged. They wore their club's navy blue leotards and white peds, had their hair brushed, parted, and braided, and a few wore yarn ties in their braids. So far, however, despite the barker's efforts, no one seemed to have noticed them. Sissy feared that if they stood here much longer, someone would pin a Best Pig ribbon on one of them.

The girls and their coach had spread red exercise mats over the platform and set up a long balance beam; it was the only equipment they had had room for. They were merely a last-day, fill-in act at the fair.

1

Waiting restlessly at the front of the platform, they stole glances at each other, twisted nervously at fingers and cuffs, and tugged at their leotards. Sissy prayed that the barker would attract enough onlookers soon so that they could start their gymnastics demonstration. She realized now that it was not the best time for an act — the last hour of the last day of a fair.

At many booths, carpenters were drawing nails and stacking plywood partitions on the ground. Animals were being hauled away in trucks and trailers. Artists were packing up exhibits, and boxes of delicious-looking fudge that in actuality tasted like plastic were being shipped off to some other fair.

Now the straw-hatted barker with sleeve garters and a cane tried again, prowling back and forth before the line of girls and their little blonde coach with his microphone. He stabbed the cane at a passing woman.

"Excuse me, madam — what's the hurry? Slow down and see the show! Nothing to lose, everything to win — "

"This is awful!" Sissy's friend, Andrea Packwood, whispered to her, as weary fairgoers glanced at the girls but kept on shuffling through the mulch of sawdust and mustardy hot-dog wrappers. Small, fussy children in funny hats, licking frozen-sherbet sticks, stared groggily, like sleepwalkers, at the idle gymnasts.

"Hey, hey, *hey*!" chortled the announcer. "You, lady — you look like a responsible mother. What are *you* going to say when somebody asks, Where is your darling daughter tonight? Out whooping it up? No, ma'am! She's going to be at Bonnie Walker's gymnastics club developing her muscles!"

Not *muscles*, mister, Sissy thought bleakly, looking at Holly Webb. Who needs big muscles? Not muscles, but *skills*!

But no one seemed to care what her daughter was going to be developing; the people kept trudging by. Sissy stole a look at Bonnie Walker, their coach, who stood small but erect in a red exercise suit at the head of the line. She looked embarrassed, and Sissy knew she was on the point of saying,

"All right, girls, let's stack the mats and go home."

On impulse, Sissy darted to Bonnie's side.

"Bonnie? Why don't you take the mike and just *say* it, huh? And we'll start our backsprings. Then they've *got* to notice. He's *never* going to catch anybody with that stuff."

Bonnie nibbled a thumbnail, and gave a

3

nod. "All right! But remember — only three back handsprings, or you'll flip right off the platform. Then Holly with the floor exercise, and you afterward on the beam. Hit the springboard as hard as you can, because this floor's *dead*."

Bonnie murmured behind her hand to the announcer, while Sissy returned to tell the girls, mimicking their old coach, Ruby Heinrich: "Okay, ladies — chewing gum behind your ears and hit the mats. This is it!"

The girls lined up, Holly Webb first because she was the tallest and would do the first routine, then Sissy. In age, the girls ranged from ten to fifteen, and not every one represented the cream of the Butterflies Gymnastics Club. They happened to be the only ones the coach had been able to round up this afternoon, when the phone call came to the gym that there was a chance to fill in for a canceled act. It was an opportunity to promote the club itself, and gymnastics as a sport.

The barker presented the microphone to Bonnie like a nosegay, then playfully dropped his straw hat on her head. Holly led the other girls to the front of the judging stand, where, earlier this week, pigs had

4

paraded and square dancers had whirled. A small boy thrilled Sissy by yelling excitedly as Holly began her series of back handsprings. Sissy was next, and she tucked in her chin and squared her shoulders.

"The secrets of tumbling," Bonnie's voice came over the loudspeaker, "are thousands of years old. Most kings had their court tumblers. Children are natural tumblers, and perhaps many centuries ago some especially talented child, with a little extra courage — "

Sissy ran forward, and did a roundoff, which reversed her direction and put her in position for her back handsprings. Now children were tugging their parents to a halt. She had a glimpse of the nucleus of an audience forming as she whipped back into her three handsprings. A small figure in blue with white peds, she spun like a propeller, finished with her arms raised, smiled, and trotted to the end of the line. Her dark hair was braided and fixed in little loops like handles at the sides of her head. Small colored butterflies were sewn around the neck of her leotard.

Andrea went next. Sissy thought unhappily, She's *got* to lose some weight! She could hear her hands and feet punching the boards. Meanwhile, Bonnie continued her spiel. Two or three dozen people had collected.

"For many years, women's gymnastics were the same as men's. Women and girls tried unsuccessfully to perform tricks they weren't strong enough for. Then the sport began to change into the women's activity it is now, with more elegant tumbling moves, and dance elements in which we can be feminine *and* athletic. The Butterflies' own Holly Webb, fourteen, will now do the floor exercise for you. Since there isn't enough space, she'll perform an abbreviated version of the regular routine."

As the girls finished their backflips and re-formed in line, Holly took her position in a corner, a pretty blonde teenager with animated features, Sissy could see her plugging herself into some special source of energy. At the gym, Holly was famous for loafing, and arriving late from beach parties or cheerleader practice. But the chance to perform for an audience always inspired her.

She executed a line of back handsprings down one side of the mat, then did a stag leap, and turned to start diagonally across the mats. Very neatly she turned a front handspring, crossed the back of the platform with little ballet gallop steps, and rose to a handstand.

"The gymnast has a minute and forty seconds to complete a routine," said Bonnie. "It's always done to music, but today Holly's just — well, she's probably humming 'Windmills' to herself."

More onlookers had been attracted, and Sissy patted her hands together in pleasure. She rehearsed in her mind her run-on mount to the balance beam, and the first few moves.

"At about the time these other changes were taking place, the parallel bars became the exciting event it is today. One bar was raised, the other lowered, and they became the *uneven* parallel bars. We call them the 'unevens.' I wish we'd had time and space to set up the bars for a demonstration, but the gym is open six days a week to anyone interested in learning more about gymnastics."

Holly finished her routine with a final pose, and ran, to light clapping, back to the others. Suddenly, Andrea nudged Sissy's elbow.

"Look who's out there!" she hissed.

Sissy searched through the interested faces and felt a small shock of displeasure. A very short, compact girl of twelve with dark, curly hair stood there with a boy of thirteen who wore a military-school uniform. He, too, had curly black hair and ripe features, and his unbuttoned tunic gave him the air of a bored young dictator. The girl was Juno Heinrich, daughter of their old coach and a very talented gymnast. Her brother, Harry, home for the summer, was noted mainly for his big mouth and his arrogance.

Their mother owned the gymnastics school, fifteen miles from Meadowdale, which Sissy had quit last year, accidentally taking eighteen other dissatisfied girls with her to Bonnie's. Ruby Heinrich, Juno's mother, had never forgiven her!

Bonnie spoke to the girls and they rolled the long, spidery balance beam into position for Sissy. It had already been raised to the proper height, about four feet. It was over sixteen feet long and almost four inches wide, and a few years ago it had seemed to Sissy as dangerous as a patched plank over a wild river. But now she was able to shut out her fears and concentrate on the moves. Bonnie moved a stubby springboard, called a Reuther board, into place, and Sissy positioned it exactly where she needed it for her mount. She addressed the beam, chin tucked in; and just as she was tightening up for her takeoff, she heard Harry call:

"We heard they were going to judge the pigs over here. Are them the pigs?"

Sissy turned and put her fists on her hips, glaring at him. Juno had pressed her hand over her mouth to repress her laughter. Some people were staring indignantly at Harry, while others grinned. Then Sissy heard Bonnie saying,

"We have a question from Mr. Harry Heinrich. I'm glad you asked, because they asked me to tell you that you won first prize for best boar. Your ribbon is being held over by the hog trough."

The announcer bent down to the microphone to say,

"Which just shows to go you that gymnastics also develops a quick wit! Let's hear it for Bonnie Walker!"

While they were clapping, Sissy started off, before anything else could happen. She hit the springboard hard, but even so her foot barely cleared the beam as she rose to hold a squat position on both feet for an instant. Then she rose to an arabesque on the right leg, her arms raised vertically, held it a moment, and took her running steps to a split leap.

"Confidence and courage are key to good beam work," Bonnie explained. "It's been called 'elevated floor exercise.' This means that the gymnast is required to perform almost the same movements as in the floor routine, but on a four-inch-wide beam. She is not permitted to pause for longer than a pose requires."

Sissy worked with a sense of frustration, for her concentration had been sapped. She kept waiting for one of the rotten Heinrich kids to interrupt again. After a minute and a half of sure but uninspired beam work, her peds squeaking on the wood, she made a simple wendy dismount, and smiled her appreciation for the applause.

The sun was nearing the blue silhouette of the hills to the west; a chilliness was flowing in over the town from the Pacific Ocean, a few miles away. Bonnie Walker tied the gymnastics story into a neat parcel, and said:

"That completes our little show-and-tell. I want to emphasize that it's a sport where most girls can do well, if they work hard. All girls can develop strength and grace, even if they never become champions. There are several gymnastics clubs in Humboldt County. Are there any questions?"

Juno yelled, "I've got a question!" and Bonnie nodded at her. "What's the biggest club in the county?"

Bonnie hesitated, and Sissy scampered to the mike and cried into it,

"Your mother's, probably — Haskell's Raskells. And the biggest mouths at the fair are yours and Harry's! But biggest isn't necessarily best. So look over all the clubs before you decide on one for your daughters, ladies and gentlemen!"

The crowd applauded.

Now I'm really in the soup with the Heinrichs! Sissy knew.

Saturday Sundae

Sissy and her father were the only residents of a small hotel at the upper end of town. It was called the Mark Twain Hotel, and for many a rainy Meadowdale winter and bright or foggy summer, it had stood at the main intersection of town, its doors locked and its windows shrouded with grime. The Mark Twain had been constructed entirely of redwood logged only miles away, and had the simple architecture of a telephone booth — lofty but narrow. It was adorned, however, with every gimcrack and fiddle-faddle known to the sleeve-gartered carpenters of the Victorian era: scrolls, spindles, cornices, skylights. Men who wore aprons and derby hats had built the hotel, her father told Sissy; artisans who had worked like surgeons, on patients of wood.

And it stood proudly; decade after decade it stood. But the little dairy town failed to grow much between 1870 and 1970, and the twenty guest rooms often stood empty except for antique bedroom sets. Finally, it closed. An old dairy farmer named Mr. Olsen bought it as an investment. He stored feed in the lobby, and for one cold, rainy week he kept a new calf in the dining room. A calf in the very room where Mark Twain had cracked jokes with reporters, on a lecture tour through Northern California!

Then, two years ago, Sissy and her father hit town, and Mr. Benedict, a cabinetmaker, began buying small houses, renovating them with skill and love, and reselling them. Every time he sold one, he and his daughter moved to a new Victorian ghost house, which he immediately set to work on. (At school, on Sissy's records, a secretary finally scrawled: *Gypsy*, where it asked for her address.)

Mr. Olsen admired these shining memories of earlier days. "Make me feel like a boy again," he told them. "Just an idea, but how much would it cost to fix up the Mark Twain? Maybe I could sell it to some easterner."

He still thought all the money in the United States was in the East. It certainly wasn't in Meadowdale.

Sissy's father measured, estimated, and prayed, and Mr. Olsen decided to try it. "Knock off five hundred dollars, and you and your daughter can live in it till it's finished."

So they started ten months ago. It was now about twenty percent completed. Slow, slow; but thorough. You couldn't do hasty work on a Swiss watch, could you?

The morning after the demonstration, Sissy was doing a pancake split on a blue mat just inside the street door. The high-ceilinged lobby smelled like a sawmill, rich with cedar fir, and redwood perfume. Fine sawdust had settled on Mr. Benedict's intricate woodworking machinery, on stacks of lumber, and the huge grandfather's clock that made hollow clucking sounds like a giant wooden hen. The life story of a famous woman gymnast was spread open and on the mat beside Sissy.

Someone darkened the street door, and she looked up. It was Andrea, in jeans, tennis shoes, and green leotard-top. She came in, handed Sissy a paper napkin, and gave an embarrassed squirm of her pudgy body.

"It's from Juno!" she said.

Sissy turned it over. "What is it?"

"An invitation. I was just passing the ice cream store, and Harry brought it out. Juno's there now with some of the Raskells."

The writing was on the inside, and read:

HEY HOW ABOUT JOINING US FOR SUNDYS AT THE DIDDY WIDDLE?

LOVE, JUNO

" 'Love!' Huh!" Sissy snorted. " 'Joining them,' huh? Joining is something Daddy does with two pieces of wood and some glue. What's the idea? She knows we don't eat ice cream. We'll have to think about this."

She marked her place in the book with the napkin, shifted from the pancake split into a sitting position, and extended her legs before her. Andrea watched with envy as she drew up her right knee, raised her right arm and, by a trick of timing and strength which defied the law of gravity, went up and over, backward, into an effortless walkover onto her feet. The trick was called a valdez. Many tricks were called after gymnasts who invented them.

"You do a valdez so neat!" said Andrea wistfully.

"So do you, Andrea. Only lately you're

15

slower on your takeoff because of your, um, extra weight." Sissy dusted herself off. She wore a white tee shirt with faded red sleeves, and an old leotard. She pulled on some ragged jeans and even more ragged red tennis shoes. Her quick blue eyes were still narrowed in thought.

"You know what she's doing, don't you?" she said. "She's trying to sabotage us because we quit her mother's club. Listen — if we go, you mustn't eat anything rich."

"I *know*!" Andrea said, almost tearful as she squeezed a handful of flesh from her waist. "Bonnie told me to always carry some carrot sticks or a peeled cucumber in my purse to snack on." And she patted her fat clutch purse to prove it.

"Just *carrying* a cucumber won't do it," Sissy told her. "Oh, well — I've got a feeling she really wants to say something to us, so we'd better go. I'll leave a note for Daddy."

She dodged through the litter of boards and machines and antique furniture covered with drop cloths, pausing to pick up a triangular scrap of plywood to scribble on. She wrote a message on the satiny wood with a ballpoint, and left it propped against a Tiffany lamp.

The Hotel Must Die!

As she stepped into the street, a fresh breeze brushed her face. She sniffed it like a pony, ecstatic over its secret perfumes of hill and dale. The Mark Twain stood just under a wooded hill, where the village ended. Beyond were hills, forests, pockets of meadow, and the ocean. The sea breezes arrived here first, laden with the resinous smells of the fir groves they had combed on their way from the Pacific. Pastures lapped the little town, so that it seemed to float in a sea of grass, in which the dairy ranches about it looked like boats riding at anchor.

Sissy treasured it all, like pictures in an album — town, hills, grass, smells, river, cows in the meadow. But in the back of the album was a grim and fading snapshot of a gray-walled prison — the big city they had

17

fled from: Cement City, she and her father called it. It refused to fade completely. Sometimes, even, it grew sharper than the pictures around her, when her father sighed and said,

"Don't know what we'll do when I run out of houses to rebuild, Princess. I'm getting most of the good cabinet work, but even so — pretty small burg."

She would wither inside if they went back to Cement City. Her father had been miserable there, short-tempered and glum. And it was in Cement City that her mother had walked out of their lives — just packed up in the middle of the night and left for a career in ballet! In the Corpus Christi Ballet and Barrel-Stave Company, her father said bitterly.

The girls turned the corner and started down Main Street. The little town was spread below them, the street lined with quaint Victorian buildings, most of them gleaming with paint and decorated with scrollwork. But halfway down the block, on the far side of the street, there was a gap like a missing tooth: a building had been demolished here and the splintered remains trucked away to the dump.

18

"Haskell Heinrich, the great wrecker," said Sissy, bitterly. "I'm glad my father is a builder, not a wrecker."

"Juno thinks he's big stuff," sniffed Andrea. "Just because they're rich — " She broke off and nudged Sissy. They stared at the girl in jeans who had sauntered from the Diddy Widdle, just ahead of them. It was Juno. She had a vivid, brash prettiness, and the muscular swagger of a tumbler. She had, in fact, been a California tumbling champion before she was nine. She saw them and called,

"Hurry up! Kelly's already making your sundaes."

"Remember, now," Sissy muttered to Andrea.

"But they're already made!"

"Don't eat it. Let it melt. She knows we don't eat that stuff."

Juno grinned at them and went inside. The entrance was an alcove set back between two display windows. On the right was a collection of dusty antiques — old crimping irons, a churn, flatirons. In the other window was a dusty, unappetizing orgy of imitation sundaes, sodas, and malted milks. They had probably been there since 1930.

Inside, antique sewing machines had been made into tables, and the two young waitresses wore old-fashioned gowns. Two tables had been pushed together to form a single long one. Harry lolled at the far end, looking like a teenage general, in his military-school dress blues. Juno stood at the street-end of the table, nibbling a fingernail in thought.

"Let's see — why don't you sit at my left, Andrea? And Sissy, why don't you sit at my right?"

What's the catch? Sissy wondered. The seating plan put her beside Lori Long, and Andrea beside Lori's twin sister, Liz. They were identical twins, absolutely undistinguishable except for the names stitched on their pockets. A dark girl called Gazelle Stubbs, at Harry's right, completed the party. Everyone had a tulip-shaped glass of ice cream streaked with fudge, cherry syrup, and whipped cream and nuts. The whole ice cream parlor reeked of sweets, and Sissy hoped Andrea had the moral fiber to match the temptation.

"Let's go, Kelly!" Juno called to the young woman who was concocting the sundaes.

Kelly Mills, too, was a gymnast, and she wrinkled her nose at Juno, and said, "Cool it, big shot." When she was off duty, she hand-spotted at Bonnie's gym — gave girls a hand-boost in difficult tricks, and helped out in general. Suddenly Juno clapped her hands together.

"Hey, Mom's getting a new coach! He's in college, and he nearly made the Olympics! His name's Ted."

Sissy tried to keep her disappointment from showing. Good coaches made good gymnasts, and a near-Olympics coach on the Raskells staff sounded like bad news.

"Just for the summer?" she asked, hopefully.

"He's not sure yet," said Juno enigmatically.

Kelly thumped the sundaes before the girls. She was small and trim, her fair hair worn in a bun, her features calm and Slavic, making her look like an Iron Curtain gymnast.

"What this town needs," she stated, "is a training table. How's the diet going, Andrea?"

Andrea, blushing, dug a booklet from her purse. "I was going to see if it allows you to have a little, you know, light dessert once in a while," she mumbled.

"Oh, live a little, Andrea!" cried Juno, gaily.

The other three Raskells laughed and rattled their spoons against their dishes as they dug in once more.

"Well, *I* can tell you, Andrea," said Kelly, "that all you'll find under H, for Hot Fudge Sundae, is H-Two-O."

"*I'll* look!"

Juno snatched the booklet from Andrea.

"Here y'are! 'Sauerkraut!' How about a sauerkraut soda? Or, here: *'Fish!'* No, no! *'Clams!'* "

"Clams!" squealed Lori Long, who like her sister was tall, without an eighth-inch of flab anywhere. "Carry some clams in your coin purse to munch on!"

"No — a warm flounder!" Liz cried.

Sissy swung on Juno a scornful look that would have frozen a thermometer. She held it there until Juno had to meet her gaze, and she drilled her contempt into Juno's somewhat frog-like eyes until Juno glanced away, abashed. Maybe now she'll get down to business, she thought.

She did.

Juno turned to Andrea, at her left, and laid her hand on the pudgy little gymnast's

22

arm. "Andrea, honey, will you tell me something?" she said, in a voice as sickly-sweet as hot fudge, and as treacherous. She sounded as though she'd just heard that Andrea was dying.

Andrea tucked a wisp of brown hair behind her ear. "What's that?"

"How come you quit my mom's club?"

Andrea shot a look of alarm at Sissy. She dabbed at her sundae. "Well, uh-what I said when I quit. My mother thought we got home too late from workouts."

"I don't see why your mother should have been worried," replied Juno, "because *my* mother drives the bus. Is that why all eighteen of you Butterflies switched to Bonnie's?"

The first spoonful of ice cream went into Andrea's mouth, leaving a drop of fudge on her lower lip. She nodded, seeming to draw courage from its sweetness. "I don't know about the others," she said, "but that was why *I* quit. That, and the bus fare — "

"Big deal," jeered General Harry. "Fifty cents a day."

"— Is ten dollars a month, as I remember," said Sissy. In contempt, she pushed the dish of ice cream away. "As a matter of fact, Juno," she said coldly, "we quit because it's a lot better deal at Bonnie's. She's a real hot-dog dance instructor, *and* gymnast."

It was out! The girls gasped. Gazelle's spoon clattered on the tabletop, and she covered her discomfiture by blurting: "I think Ruby's the greatest coach in the world, myself!"

Sissy said: "Ho! If she was, you wouldn't still be getting bruises trying to do a backward walkover on the beam."

Gazelle's mouth fell open in shock. She looked at Juno, who stiffened like a cat.

"Oh, is *that* why you quit?" she said. "Because Gazelle couldn't do a back walkover?"

"No. Because *I* couldn't. But I can now. I can do a back handspring."

Juno turned her head on one side and closed one eye. "Oh now wait! *On the beam?*"

"On the beam!"

"I've got to see that someday. Is that the only reason?"

"No, just one of them. Because let's face it, Juno, your mother doesn't know much about dance, and that's as important as tumbling. The floor-ex and beam events are fifty percent dance."

Liz Long winked at her sister. "I guess Bonnie Walker knows dance, all right."

Lori giggled. "Especially" — keeping her face down — "belly dancing."

Sissy turned on her. "What's that supposed to mean?"

"Oh, nothing."

"Come on, what's it mean?"

"She means," Juno said, "that Bonnie was arrested once for taking her dress off and belly dancing in a bar."

"That's a lie!" Sissy said. "Just a cheap shot, and it sounds like slander, to me. She could sue you."

Juno smilingly ate the cherry from her sundae, which she had been saving to the last, and said mysteriously:

"Bet I know something that isn't a lie."

"What's that?" Sissy challenged. "What?" Yet an ice cube had begun to form in her abdomen, as she thought, Here it comes!

"My dad's bought the Mark Twain Hotel, and he's going to demolish the old eyesore and build a Frosty Freeze."

The news landed on Sissy like a tombstone. As a dazed boxer weaves, she tried to cover up. "You're making it up. I don't believe you."

"Suit yourself," said the General, "but you'd better start packing. He made Olie

Olsen a final offer last night, and Olie can't refuse. He's broke."

All the girls were glancing surreptitiously at Sissy. She was hurt and scared, and they all knew it. "The council wouldn't let him," she said blankly.

"What council?" jeered Harry.

"The town council. They — there's a bill to preserve historic landmarks. After what your father did to the old carriage works."

"Well, it hasn't passed yet. And demolition is Dad's profession — tearing down rotten old eyesores."

Sissy repeated something she had heard her father say after Haskell Heinrich demolished the old carriage works across the street: "Tearing down landmarks is the whole town's business. Mark Twain stayed three days at the hotel once. That's when they changed the name. It used to be the Hotel Denmark."

"I doubt that Mark Twain story," Juno said airily. "Kelly, another sundae for Andrea."

"No, I — I really — "

The street door opened and a big, florid-faced man looked in. "Sissy Benedict? On the double." It was Chief Packwood, Andrea's father, head of the two-man police department. "You're wanted at the hotel, sweetie. Code Six! Olie Olsen hailed me as I passed the hotel."

The bad news was confirmed.

Sissy tried to pull herself together, but she was scared. It was still possible — her father had said he'd buy the hotel himself if . . . if he could swing it. He'd said, This is a jewel of Victorian architecture, a national treasure. . . . She thought of one of Heinrich's red wrecking balls plowing into its delicate matchstick structure with a splintering crash.

She got up. "Thank you. Juno," she said archly, "did you ever learn to do a Diddy Widdle cartwheel?"

"What's that?" scoffed Juno.

"Through the door, and finish with an aerial."

Juno ran a calculating glance toward the door. "I can if you can."

Sissy could do cartwheels right down a crack in the lobby flooring, and there was a line here in the asphalt tile that she could follow straight out the door. Handing her clutch purse to Andrea, she took a couple of steps in the direction of the door; then, saying the trick in her mind like a poem, *one-two-three-four*, *hand-hand-foot-foot*, she did two cartwheels, seeing the tables and chairs upend themselves, come back, upend themselves, and come back again. And finally, she half-twisted onto the sidewalk in an aerial cartwheel, landing on her feet with her arms raised and looking back through the door into the ice cream parlor.

She heard Andrea and Kelly applauding.

Juno Heinrich got up from the table and Sissy saw her hesitate, eyeing the clearance in the doorway carefully. Then she rolled sideward in a fast cartwheel — a little too fast. It was a broken one-two-three-four, with a side-sway that caused her foot to hit the jamb of the door. But she finished in a good aerial, to the *yays* and clapping of the Raskells.

Now, Sissy knew, she'll practice and practice on that until she beats me or gets calluses on her hands trying. But if we have to move, and I never compete against her again; or if Daddy has to take a job in the city, she knows her foot hit and mine didn't.

Small comfort.

Take It or Leave It!

Mr. Olsen's pickup truck was parked crookedly before the hotel when Sissy and Andrea arrived. Its heavy tires were clotted with mud, and a tan calf standing patiently between the high board sides of the truck bed gazed back at them with melting, beautiful eyes. The animal had the calm look of Olie himself.

Sissy stopped, and with a lump in her throat looked at the little hotel. It had stood for a century, had aged like old ivory, acquiring a special beauty; had been condemned and reprieved. And now a greedy man with a wrecking crane was going to destroy it — and replace it with a Frosty Freeze!

It was cruel. It was insane.

Andrea tugged at Sissy's sleeve. "Sissy! *What* am I going to *do*?"

"Do about what?" Sissy sniffled, reaching

up to tease a tear from the corner of her eye before it could spill. She had thought *she* was the one with the problem.

"All that ice cream I ate! When I saw it — I just couldn't — " She shook her head in despair.

"Go into the ladies room and put your finger down your throat. My father knew a jockey who used to keep his weight down that way. But don't get in the habit."

"You mean — vomit?"

"Throw it up. Otherwise" — she pinched Andrea's waist " — your personal fudge-factory will go into gear."

She faced the open door of the hotel, catching a glimpse of white drop cloths and stacked lumber inside. Okay, face the music, she thought drearily. Start packing for Cement City. But in style! She did a chassé through the door, left toe chasing right heel.

"Hi, Mr. Olsen!" she said to the old man sitting on a long, carved sofa. The cover had been thrown from it and he and her father sat there in the spice of freshly-sawn wood. Mr. Benedict had a scratch pad on his lap and was doodling on it.

"Hello, ladies," said the old dairy farmer. His face was pale from the eyebrows up, beefy-red from the brows down. A tractor-company cap lay on his lap. "Excuse the overhauls. No use me dressing like a banker, because people'd just say, 'What's that big old farmer doin' in banker's clothes?' "

Sissy smiled and sat beside him. Andrea went into the ladies room off the lobby.

"Will you tell Sissy what you just told me?" Sissy's father said. Under his yellow hard hat, his face looked stern.

"Sure," said Mr. Olsen. Sissy squirmed to get comfortable, because when Mr. Olsen told something he touched all the bases.

"I had a telephone call from Haskell Heinrich," he said, gazing straight ahead through his thick glasses. "He said he was making me a final offer. He's been finagling to buy this hotel for a year. But this time he said if I didn't take it, I could rot in cow manure — them were his words. 'Forty thousand,' he said. 'Take it or leave it, and rot in cow manure.' "

Sissy nodded. She patted her toes against the floor.

"Well, I'd have told him to go rot in manure himself, but the fact is I just sold my dairy farm. And frankly, I've had it with cow manure. And me and Hazel have made an offer on a trailer park in Modesto, and I've got to have cash. Still and all, to let that trashy Heinrich demolish this place —

"So I said, 'Give me overnight to think about it.' That was yesterday. Now I've got to say yea or nay by six o'clock tonight because they accepted our offer on the trailer park. Got to deposit the money with the bank by tonight. But I'll tell you something!"

He looked piercingly at Sissy as though there were a fly on her nose, then at Mr. Benedict in the same way. Sissy thought, He's going to say how sad he is to disappoint us.

"The people who ought to have this hotel are you two! You're a cabinetmaker, Frank, and can do right by it. You can preserve it from the wrath of Heinrich. I can just see you two here operating this hotel. The perfect team! Be cheap to operate, once it was finished; and there's a lot more tourists coming through these days. Can't you swing it somehow?"

Evidently he had said it before, because Sissy's father gazed at her with a cautious smile. "What do you think, Princess?"

In shock, she gazed around the lobby, seeing everything with new eyes as she thought of *owning* it. She heard the toilet flush, and

Andrea emerged from the rest room, pale as pork fat but looking relieved.

"Do we *have* forty thousand dollars?" she asked.

"No, but we've got twenty-two from the last house we sold, and the bank will loan fifteen on the hotel, as is. We'd be short three thousand, but Olie says he'd take a note for it."

"What's a note?" Sissy asked.

"A promise to pay. Rather have the cash," said Mr. Olsen, "but I'd take a note, due when you can pay it, if you keep up the interest."

Sissy's father took off his hard hat and parked it on Sissy's head, while he massaged his scalp with his fingertips as if to get his brain working better. Now Sissy could see only the floor, but even that was enough to tell her that they couldn't do it. Since she'd been doing the shopping, she knew how much things cost, even if you clipped the coupons out of the newspaper food section. And certainly you could not pay for a hotel with coupons.

"What would we make the loan payments with?" she asked.

"Room rents," said her father. "I could

have six rooms ready in two months, if I really cranked up now. We'd take college students and loggers first, because they wouldn't mind the sawdust and a little pounding at night. By next summer we'd have all the rooms ready. Maybe even the restaurant."

Andrea leaned toward Sissy. "Mr. Heinrich is sure going to be mad!" she whispered.

Sissy lifted off the heavy yellow helmet. Andrea was peering anxiously at her. Her father was waiting for her to speak, and Mr. Olsen was squeezing his hands together as though breaking all the bones in them. Sissy was breathless, as if it were a big moment on the balance beam. But then she pictured a red, pear-shaped iron ball roaring through the front of the hotel in a hurricane of splinters and flying glass. . . .

"Let's do it!" she said.

Mr. Olsen patted her knee. "Good girl," he said. "I asked 'em to get the papers ready at the bank. So if you're ready, Frank — "

"Ready when you are," said Sissy's father. "You're working out this afternoon, Sissy? I'll see you at dinner."

The men hurried out.

"Wow!" Andrea said numbly. "Is Mr. Heinrich ever going to be mad!"

"I'll tell you who'd be mad!" said Sissy. "Me, if he ever touched a hair of this hotel's head! This is going to serve him right!"

Funny Ankles

"Mistake Number One," a man was saying to Bonnie Walker, "was to buck Ruby Heinrich. As an old Meadowdaler, you should have known that. She was a witch even before she married a professional wrecker. Mistake Number Two was to let Sissy Benedict's father buy the Mark Twain."

"*I* couldn't keep him from buying it, Ernie!" Bonnie's voice protested. "I didn't even *know*, till Sissy told me yesterday, after he'd signed the papers."

Sissy was parking her bicycle before the gym while Bonnie and the man, Ernie — Ernie who? — conversed inside. The club was in an old church that Sissy's father had transformed into a gym. Sissy could hear the Reuther board banging and recorded piano music tinkling. On its sloping corner, the building stood tall and white, with a retaining wall to prevent it from sliding into the intersection of Redwood and Jersey streets.

Sissy took her time parking her bicycle, wanting to hear more about Mistakes Number One and Two. Clearly, they concerned her and her father.

"Maybe you couldn't stop him, Bonnie," said the man, "but Ruby thinks you went out of your way to egg him on. Ruby thinks all is not gymnastics that brings him to the United Brethren Reformed Church."

Sissy wondered, too. She knew her father carried a small newspaper picture of Bonnie in his wallet, with the caption: MEADOWDALE WOMAN OPENS GIRLS' GYM. DANCERGYMNAST RETURNS FROM EAST.

"All *is* gymnastics," Bonnie said coolly. "He charged over thirty dollars an hour to tear out pews and install floor anchors for the equipment. It's true I've waived Sissy's dues in return for part of the bill — "

"Like no dues till she's forty?" Ernie chuckled. "Anyway, he's torn the hotel out of Heinrich's hot hands, after Sissy started the shift to your club last year. Eighteen girls! *I'm* surprised that *you're* surprised that the Raskells have challenged you to a meet. I mean, you're in a war, baby."

Shocked, Sissy let go of her bike before it was properly balanced on the kick-stand. It toppled against the bicycle next to it, which fell against the next, and in seconds the whole line of wheels and frames had crashed to the sidewalk.

A young man looked out the door. Sissy had seen him around town, and did not know his name. But you certainly couldn't miss him! Like an old-time gambler, he wore a black coat, derby, and carried a gold-headed cane. A dandy, they used to call them. He had a good-natured, ruddy face, but wore enormous mirror-lensed sunglasses that made him look like some kind of bug. Like a man removing his hat when he met a lady, he took off the glasses, and she saw he had lively blue eyes.

"You see?" he said, glancing back at Bonnie. "Heinrich's ace wrecker has already arrived."

"That's Sissy Benedict," Bonnie said, in a low tone that suggested that the less anybody said to her, the better. "Hurry up, Sissy — we've started warmups."

Sissy tried to set the bikes up again, but there were at least a dozen of them, and in despair she darted up the wooden steps, carrying her red tote bag. The man blocked the door with his cane.

"Hi, Sissy! Got a minute? I'm Ernie Ware

— sports reporter for the Eureka *Tribune*.
I'm doing a piece on girls' gymnastics in
Humboldt County."

"Oh," Sissy said. She squirmed past him.
Inside the small vestibule, girls' clothing
hung on wall hooks or lay on the floor. Beyond the vestibule was a big, raftered hall
where people used to come to pray, but
where now gymnasts came to practice. A
few rows of pews had been left in the rear
for spectators, but most of the floor was
taken up by a large blue mat, and the
gleaming bars and uprights of gymnastics
equipment. Girls in leotards and exercise
suits were jogging around the hall doing
warmup laps.

Sissy sat on the floor and unlaced her tennis shoes. She wore an old leotard under her
jeans, and was ready when she pulled the
jeans off. She wore knee-length socks, which
were supposed to help prevent shin splints.
On the front of her blue tee shirt she had
embroidered a happy-looking orange mon-
ster. Bonnie stood before her, blocking her
from Ware's presence. He held a thick pad of
paper in one hand and was writing on it.

"Let's go, Sissy," Bonnie urged. "We're
starting a new warmup routine today. More
laps and strength exercises. Everybody in

this club is as weak as a kitten." She was very small and trim, about the size, Sissy guessed, that she herself would be someday. Not very big.

"You're too hard on them, Bonnie," Ware said. "Why, I'll bet Sissy can do twenty pushups."

Sissy glanced up. "I did seventy one day!" she said. "But that's more because I'm light, than strong."

"Seventy! Juno can only do fifty. I was up at Redwood College this morning, where they work out. I suppose that would give you an advantage over her in some of the stunts, wouldn't it?"

"Will you knock it off, Ernie?" Bonnie pleaded. "I won't have my girls dragged into a feud. Sissy's a good little gymnast, but so is Juno — and a lot of the other girls. Juno was a tumbling champion when she was nine. Come on, Sissy — "

"Wait!" Ware said, with a wink at Sissy. "Don't you want to hear what Ruby Heinrich said this morning?"

"No," Bonnie said. But Sissy did, and she waited.

"When I told her I was going to interview you, she said, 'Don't expect to learn much. Bonnie Walker's not teaching the girls anything they couldn't learn on their front lawns.' And Juno said, 'Bonnie's not a gymnast, she's just a tap dancer with funny ankles.' "

Bonnie indignantly looked down at her ankles, and Ware guffawed. "Don't let them rattle you, Bonnie. Your ankles are great. Anyway, I gave you a chance to get even. I said, 'Why don't you challenge the Butterflies to a meet, and settle who's best?' "

"Thanks a lot," Bonnie said, heatedly. And she started pushing Sissy into the gym. At the far end of the hall, near the little stage with its pulpit, the big blue mat stretched almost from wall to wall. Down the right-hand wall ran a string of red mats that ended at a leather vaulting horse. The uneven parallel bars stood like a chrome-and-wood drying rack at the right, and on the left a half-dozen long practice beams lay on floor mats, while two standard balance beams, four feet high, were aligned near the wall. Light fell through the stained glass windows in blue, green, and ruby patterns on the floor.

"A little two-club meet," Ware said. "What do you say?"

"I say it's a grudge match, and no thank you."

"Ruby suggested two weeks from Saturday."

"I'm suggesting that you get lost. I'm training gymnasts, not gladiators. We have oodles of practice meets coming up this fall, and we're not going to rush the season."

Ware chewed his pencil and watched the girls jogging past in a bouquet of colored leotards, tee shirts, exercise suits, and plain sweatsuits. "Maybe I shouldn't have brought it up," he said. "Because if you duck out now, it'll seem like you lack confidence in your girls — or your own coaching. . . ."

Bonnie went closer to him, smiling wickedly. "I'll bet you hadn't thought of that, had you? Oh, no! Or that if we agree to a match, and lose, they'll say I'm not teaching the girls anything. And then I won't get any new students after school starts."

"*Are* you teaching them anything?" Ware asked. "No hard feelings, but as a reporter I have to ask these questions — "

Sissy spoke up. "She's the best coach I've ever had, and I've had a dozen." When Ware looked at her with amusement, she suddenly realized that he was playing them both like fish.

"What's she teaching you, Sissy?" he asked.

42

"The basics," Sissy said promptly. "Ruby's always starting somebody on an optionals routine before she's even got her compulsories down pat. So the girl keeps taking falls, and loses confidence. But Bonnie won't let us try any advanced tricks till we're ready."

"Let me get this straight. The compulsories are tricks everybody has to do?"

"Yes. Every girl in the U.S. has to do the same ones. They're in a book. After she knows them, she and her coach work out optional routines. They're the hard ones."

"So what we've got here," Ware said hopefully, "is a war over coaching philosophies!"

Bonnie picked lint off her sleeve. "Every coach has her own methods," she said.

"Then why not prove whose method is best, with a meet?"

"Because that's *not* what it would prove! Ruby Heinrich's got twice as many girls as I have, including some really fine gymnasts like Liz and Lori Long. — Well, Ernie," she said in exasperation, "since you leave me no choice, I'll put it to the girls. But on our terms: compulsories only, and a limit of a dozen girls — four in each skills level."

Bonnie told the girls, and they were all excited over the meet. But Bonnie looked them over critically as they stood chattering.

"I don't know whether you realize it," she said, "but most of you aren't even ready. People get lazy in summer. You'll have to work, and I'll test you the day before the meet and pick the twelve best.

"Get going on warmups, now. Fifteen laps, then twenty minutes of stretches — splits, back-bends, shoulder stretches — every muscle you've got. Then a half hour of vaulting. And last but not least, a complete strength circuit. Go!"

While they worked, Ware cruised around shooting pictures. Sissy was sure he did not really know what he was seeing. When he took pictures of her doing her floor routine, he probably did not realize he was seeing the worst part of her gymnastics work. It was on the beam and the floor that your faults were most obvious, because mere quickness and flash could not disguise lack of amplitude and grace.

She had not worried about grace until recently. Gymnastics had come naturally to her. From the time she was five, her mother had dumped her in every gymnastics class she could find; later, when she herself got involved in ballet, she had dragged Sissy along to rehearsals. Sissy would practice by herself, out of the way.

So Sissy had a head start. She zipped through Class III and Class II. Well before most girls, she was working on Class I routines. Then one day, when she was in Haskell's Raskells, and coming along fast, Ruby had said in her jeering way,

"You think gymnastics is easy, don't you? You'll find out, sweetheart! Just wait till you bang your nose into a block! Then you'll learn why girls drop out."

Ruby was a real sweetheart herself. In a way, she had caused Sissy to bang nose-first into her first Block.

Mental blocks were not things you could solve by reading a book; often even a coach could not help. In Sissy's case, it was more of a feeling she had about herself than an outright failure in some area. She would zip through her difficult optionals floor routine, and suddenly realize — *I'm as mechanical as a windup toy!* A gifted gymnast — an Elite, for instance — revealed grace in every move. What she revealed was stiffness.

She could not seem to break through to the elegance she strove for. She would finish a perfect floor routine, look at Bonnie for approval, and catch a frown. Or Kelly would pat her shoulder and say,

"A little stiff. Think about hands and fingers and toes. Make them work. Think about elegance."

She thought about it all the time, but she was still wooden.

After the floor work, she wandered over to the uneven parallel bars and waited with Christi Haddon. Christi was older than Sissy, and very attractive. She had just done her unevens routine, and looked discouraged. Christi wore her old SCATS shirt, which was significant, in a way. The SCATS were a famous club she'd belonged to in the Los Angeles area. But that was two years ago, and she was, in a sense, like an old soldier still wearing his uniform. Christi needed the shirt for reassurance.

Kelly signaled to Holly Webb, and the girl started her routine on the parallel bars. She did a kip catch up to the high bar, then a kip cast into a sole circle, her hands and feet on the bar, that ended with her lying out flat, face up and looking at the ceiling of the church. She gave a swift twist of her body, attempting to flip over and change to an overhand grip. But she failed to complete the turn, and her left hip crashed into the bar. She jumped off, rubbing her hip and frowning.

"The bar's loose, Kelly," she complained. "Can't we tighten the cables?"

Kelly tugged at a cable. "They're all right. Try it again. You made your twist too late."

Christi whispered to Sissy: "It would help if she did some strength exercises, too."

Sissy nodded. Holly's problem was that she was a queen bee — into everything, Girl Scouts, cheerleading, class treasurer. And every sunny day she and a bunch of friends got somebody's mother to drive them five miles to the beach. But in gymnastics, if you missed a single day's practice, the whole club could see it the next time you worked out.

Holly faced the low bar again, moistening her lips and preparing for her mount. Christi said with a sigh:

"It's kind of discouraging. . . ."

Sissy looked at her. "What is?"

"That I was better two years ago than I am now."

"No, you weren't. You've just reached a plateau. Everything's harder in Class I. But all of a sudden you'll break through and really start improving. I wish I looked as good on the unevens as you do."

"But how'd you like to be as clumsy on the mat as I am? Thump, thump, thump! — here comes Christi!" She glanced around uneasily. "Don't you think Ruby kind of *explained* the moves better?" she asked.

Sissy laughed. "All she ever explained to me was that tuition and bus fare were due on the first of the month. Why don't you tell Bonnie you need extra help?"

"Because I don't really understand what she says! It's like she was talking another language. — Oh, well, maybe I'll ask again."

Sissy hoped she would. For the truth was that Christi had an advanced case of what Sissy feared she was coming down with. Though she was strong, quick, and precise, she too was rather wooden in the grace elements.

Big Man, Little Man

"I have a dream," said Haskell Heinrich.
"Of knocking down every rat-infested,
roach-ridden woodpile in Northern California. Of selling the old hardwood to artistic
nuts to make wood carvings out of. Of building modern concrete structures on the land
where these Victorian firetraps were taking
up space. That's my dream, Benedict. And
nobody's going to get in the way of it!"

He was a big, blue-jawed man in a forest-
green logger's shirt, tailored green pants,
and silver hard hat. He sat on the ornate
sofa in the Mark Twain lobby with a stink-
ing cigar in his teeth which he worked restlessly back and forth. His hands gripped his
knees. Like a logging truck, he throbbed
with power.

It was the cigar which had told Sissy he
was there. She was in the upstairs hall after
dinner, helping her father determine

whether the floor really tilted from north to south. Sissy held a chalk line against the baseboard at the south end while her father studied the line level, a little silver tube with a window in it through which you could see a fat bubble dancing.

"Juno's father's downstairs!" she said suddenly.

"Huh? Who said so?"

"I can smell his cigar. He used to drive the bus sometimes, and it was *awful.* He must be in the lobby. Smells come up the stairs from the lobby."

Her father squinted at the bubble some more. "We have a very intricate system of drafts in this hotel," he said. "I'll put in weather-stripping before winter."

"Aren't you going down?"

"Not until he rings the bell. The sign on the reception counter says, RING BELL FOR SERVICE. He's no different from anybody else."

"Benedict! Where are you?" a bull-like voice bawled downstairs.

"Ring the bell!" Mr. Benedict called back. He scratched his neck and said to Sissy, "We've got two inches of fall from my end of the hall to your end. That's why the baseboard is so far from the floor. I thought maybe somebody had reinstalled the baseboard too high. But now I think maybe the hall's sunk."

The bell was rung vigorously. But it was one of those little teachers' desk-bells that can merely say *Ting, ting, ting*. And *ting* was not a sound a bull like Haskell Heinrich would enjoy making.

Sissy's father put on his yellow hard hat and they went down to the landing above the lobby. It was dark except for a lamp on the counter, where not a single guest had signed the register for twenty years. Much of the rest of the floor space was taken up with piles of lumber. The hotel itself was like a block of pure redwood, for redwood groves had surrounded the town in the 1860's, before the land was cleared for pasture, and as trees were felled they were made into lumber.

Heinrich stood there with both hands gripping the edge of the counter, as though he were preparing to rip it off. "Benedict!" he said. "I want to talk to you, fella."

Mr. Benedict flipped a switch that turned on some more lamps, and they went down. Sissy sat on a low pile of plywood, while the men took places at opposite ends of the long sofa, their heads lowered a bit as though

they might start butting their hard hats together suddenly.

And then Mr. Heinrich made his speech
about his dream. And he finished: "You
should have called me before you stuck your
hand into the buzz saw like this."

"Why you? I was dealing with the owner."

"But you knew I'd been bidding on the
thing, pal."

"That was Olie's business."

Heinrich examined his cigar. "All right. I
could probably get the hotel other ways, but
I'm a square shooter. I happen to know
you're operating on a shoestring. So here's
my offer: I'll give you five thousand more
than you paid."

He took a business card from his pocket,
wrote on the back of it, and handed it to
Sissy's father. "Give that to Grotty, my office manager, in the morning. He'll fix you
up."

Sissy's father laughed. "It's not for sale,
Heinrich! My daughter and I are going to
renovate and operate the Mark Twain. As
for your dream, I think you should turn
yourself in before you do permanent harm
to some little town like this."

Heinrich gazed steadily at Sissy's father.

"Sure you want to tangle with me, Benedict?"

"I don't want to tangle with anybody. I'm too busy."

"Boxers say a good big man can always beat a good little man."

Sissy's father gazed about the lobby. "Did you see any little men around here, Sissy?" he asked.

Heinrich got up. He clutched his belt with both hands, as though someone were trying to pull his trousers down. "So you think you can beat Heinrich, and your daughter thinks she can beat Juno. You dreamers!"

Mr. Benedict shrugged. "If there's anything else you want, ring the bell."

After he left, Sissy shivered. "Gee, Daddy — !"

Her father picked up a board and sighted down it as though it were a rifle. "Just his style. Forget it. All show, no go."

He went upstairs to do some more measuring. Sissy pulled a mat from the shadows and practiced handstands. She would hold a handstand for a while, then spread her legs and swing down into a straddle sit with her hands still supporting her weight and her legs parallel to the floor. But she kept hearing Heinrich saying,

"And your daughter thinks she can beat Juno!"

She was not at all sure she could beat Juno, but she was going to try. As her father was going to try to beat Heinrich. It had seemed as though he already had beaten him, but now —

The telephone on the counter rang. "Get that, will you?" her father called down.

"Hello?" Panting a little, she leaned against the counter.

"This is Haskell Heinrich. Tell your father a good big man just licked a good little man. Have him call Sid Starkey at the bank in the morning."

The receiver buzzed like a trapped bee. She blinked and hung up, rubbing her ankle with her toe.

"Who is it?" Her father was standing above her on the railed gallery.

"Mr. Heinrich." Sissy realized she had just heard the deep voice of doom. "He says to call Sid Starkey at the bank in the morning."

"I'll call him now — at home."

Her father looked up a number and dialed it. "Sid? Frank Benedict. Have you heard from the Red Ball Express?"

He listened, gazing around the shadowed lobby absent-mindedly. "Un-huh. I see. You sold Heinrich the note Olie left for collection? What I don't get is how you could do it, if the note belonged to Olie?"

He listened some more. "Ah-ha. Olie was still short of cash, so he sold you the note. And you sold it to Heinrich, so I owe him instead of Olie. How come you did that, old buddy?"

Sissy trotted to the mat and did some more handstands while they talked.

As she understood it, the kicker was that three thousand dollars they had lacked when they signed the papers for the hotel. It was in the form of a simple loan that could be called in at any time. *At any time.* Heinrich had just bought the loan and was demanding the money. They had thirty days to raise it, and had already borrowed on everything in sight, including the hotel.

What did they have they could sell? she wondered. Not much! When her father had started buying and selling houses, he had put practically everything they owned into the business.

She swung from the handstand into another straddle sit, and found herself looking at some massive power tools. She blinked, as an idea popped in her head like a bubble.

"Daddy?" she called suddenly. "Can you borrow on your tools?"

Her father frowned, then grinned unexpectedly and fired his finger at her: *Pow!* his lips said.

"I get the picture, Sid," he told the banker calmly. "You're sorry, but he's on your board of directors, so he has the power to approve such actions. But, Sid, I'm looking at fifteen thousand dollars worth of power tools, some of them priceless antiques, some as modern as nuclear fission. How about loaning me three thousand dollars on them? And with the three thousand, I'll pay off Heinrich. Then I'll owe *you* the money, on a regular loan — not an old-fashioned, pistol-to-the-head loan like this one. Okay? Great!

"Oh, and just for luck, have the money in the form of three thousand-dollar bills. My daughter and I will pick it up sometime this week. Over and out, Sid."

Sissy's father blew on his hands. "Bedtime, Princess. Make a pretty good team, don't we? I saw the boards, you do the head work."

He threw her over his shoulder and carried her upstairs like a sack of feed.

The Iron Butterfly

The girls clustered around Bonnie, reading the caption beneath the newspaper picture of Sissy doing a dismount from the balance beam. Her short dark hair was lifted, and she wore a tense little smile, and a frown. The frown, she remembered, had been because she was afraid she had bent her knees too much in landing.

The newspaper lay on a red tumbling mat. Bonnie knelt before it, reading aloud to the girls the story about the grudge match — as the reporter had called it! — between the Raskells and the Butterflies. Holly was snapping her fingers and doing a cheerleader routine behind Sissy, who knelt beside Bonnie.

"ADMISSION WILL BE 50¢," Bonnie read, and sighed. "Oh, I wish he hadn't written all that stuff."

"I think it's neat!" Holly said.

"It's a good picture of Sissy," Christi said. "But why'd he call her 'The Iron Butterfly'?"

"I suppose because Sissy is very precise," Bonnie said. "If precision were everything, she'd be in Elite class. But look what he did to Juno! She and her mother must be furious."

Under the picture of Juno it said simply, "*Ouch!*" The camera had caught Juno rising from the beam in a valdez — up and over; her eyes were shut tightly and she looked as though she were taking a painful spill, instead of rising!

Bonnie firmly closed the newspaper, got up, and looked at the girls. "Know what they're saying now? 'We're *twice* as good as they are! We'll show them!' "

"We'll show *them*!" said Holly.

"Not with all those soft moves I've been seeing! Ruby's girls *stretch*. They block hard in their tumbling and they *use their hands* in dance! All of you are hound-dog lazy! When we finished yesterday, I could have shaken you all. Andrea flew around the un-evens like a bundle of laundry — and it's her best event! And Holly! I've seen spa-

ghetti with more strength than you're showing me. Are you doing your strength
exercises at home?"

Holly's glance wandered. "Mmm, well,
we've had house guests — "

"Fine, let's enter your house guests
against the Raskells. In the bars, it's
strength. Christi — show me the last pose
of your compulsory floor routine."

Christi did a half-kneeling pose with her
arms reaching forward. "Okay, but
stretch!" Bonnie urged. "And pull in your
stomach — No, you're not stretching! Another two inches!"

Sissy could see the pose improve as the
lines of the girl's body lengthened. "Better,"
Bonnie said. "Okay, this is for all of you:
Your name card's on the rack, and you're
saluting the judge. What are you
thinking?"

The girls looked at each other uncomfort-
ably. "Anybody?" Bonnie repeated.

Sissy giggled. "I'm thinking, 'Boy, I wish
this were over!' " The girls laughed.

"And that's just what your face tells the
judge," Bonnie said. "But Juno looks the
judge in the eye and says, 'Look at me! I'm
the best there is!' She *demands* attention.

The judge perks up a little. Juno's a terrible show-off, but so is every good gymnast."

Sissy was not sure she liked that. If you were good, wouldn't the judges see it? Bonnie was looking at her now.

"There are sports for people who don't like to be watched. If it really bothers you, maybe you should try cross-country running. Or shot-putting! Who watches a shot-putter? But if you work seven days a week on your routines, you deserve some recognition. You've taken spills, had your knees taped, and gotten bruises. Now you can do a somersault on the beam as well as you used to on the mat. Of course you want to be watched! So put your chin up and tell them, 'I'm the best!' Because if *you* don't think so, the judges certainly aren't going to."

She tossed the newspaper aside.

"We've got miles to go, and nine days to get there. I'm sorry we're into it, but maybe it's for the best. Loafers will get an extra fifteen laps, and a year in prison. Lazy fingers and toes will be cut off. Let's go!"

They warmed up for an hour, then split up into groups to take turns on the equipment. Sissy and three other girls stood at the corners of the large square mat. The old record player on the small stage made sounds like stomach rumbles as Bonnie set the needle on the record of "Windmills of Your Mind." Sissy waited, chin up, eyes on Bonnie, who had come to stand by the blue mat.

I'm good; I'm the best! Sissy tried thinking, while everything she knew about herself said, You don't even have confidence, dummy!

She rehearsed in her mind: Step right, plié, arch; step left, turn left — tuck jump. No, don't *say* it, you already know it! Free up! — stretch! — hands!

The music started. The girls came to life like a garden of bewitched statues, each executing the same movement at the same instant. On paper, the zigzag floor pattern looked like the tracks of a mouse in a maze. Sissy thought ahead: Back handsprings down the right side toward Christi's corner, then a stag leap and a left turn down the other side.

"Hands!" Bonnie was pleading. "Let's see more hands!"

Across the mat she saw Holly moving very well. Holly's inherent grace made her a natural in the dance routines, where her lack of strength held her back less. Also she liked a charged-up situation like this — she was the born show-off Bonnie was talking about. She loafed through practice sessions but found a magic source of power for a crisis.

Bonnie had taken Christi aside and was explaining something to her. Christi looked a little sulky, her head down, her gold earring studs gleaming. She nodded. Bonnie was telling her to feel and look more elegant. Christi moved back to her place and resumed the routine. The girls went diagonally across the mat in front handsprings to the far corners, turned, posed, and stepped out in little ballet steps to the next turn.

The music faded. "Places," Bonnie said. They repeated the routine, a minute and a half of turns, jumps, handstands, and walkovers. The music ended with each girl in a kneeling pose. They rose and waited.

"Okay — go on to the beam." Bonnie tweaked a finger at Sissy. "Once more, from the roundoff and back handsprings to the end. Quicker and sharper."

Sissy trotted to her place, waiting until she heard the music in her mind. She did the roundoff that put her in the square position for the back handsprings, flip-flopped briskly into the far corner, and stepped out. She ran forward into a dive tinsica — a cartwheel that ended with the gymnast on right knee, the left leg stretching forward. This was the last pose, and she held it until Bonnie came onto the mat. The other girls had drifted off to the beam.

"Was that better?" Sissy asked.

Bonnie put her hand in the middle of Sissy's back and seemed to be trying to find something in her spine. "What?" Sissy asked.

Bonnie laughed. "I thought there might be a little keyhole back there — where the key goes in to wind you up. The routine says cartwheel-to-handstand, and you cartwheel-to-handstand. It says back handspring, and you back handspring. But that's *all* you do! No bonuses."

"You mean about showing off?"

"In a way. But mostly I mean style."

Sissy passed her hand over her hair. "I guess I don't really know what style is."

"Style is how you express what you feel. That little jazz run we put into your optional routine — you've got style when you do it.

You feel light and happy, and show it. That's why I put it there — to free you up for the rest of the routine. Can you think of how you feel when you do it?"

Yes, she could. She felt happy and sure when she did it, careless and graceful as a butterfly in a garden; yet, somehow, she didn't feel that way about the other moves.

Bonnie moved her arms and shoulders and hummed a few notes of "Roller Coaster," a perky and swinging number. Sissy picked up the tune and did that part of her routine. "Good!" Bonnie said. "Now the other again, from the roundoff — "

Sissy started off, but immediately felt herself becoming stiff. She was almost in tears when she finished it, because it seemed *impossible* to feel lighthearted about something so hard to do! Bonnie nodded thoughtfully as she finished.

"All right. Now extend your arms."

Sissy stood straight, her chest lifted and her arms extended. Then she remembered *stretch*, and she reached out a little farther. "What about your hands?" Bonnie said.

Sissy pushed her hands back until her wrists ached. "You still look as though you're directing traffic. You want the longest, straightest line you can make. And your hands should be back like the tips of a bird's wings. A complete dancer dances with her hands."

The girls from the unevens group were clustering about, listening to Bonnie and looking at Sissy. She felt clumsy and defeated. Bonnie gave her a pat on the seat.

"Work on your isolation routine at home. One shoulder at a time — the head — the hips — the hands. Someday, when you really feel like showing off, you'll know what I mean about style."

But right now, as she awaited her turn on the balance beam, Sissy felt like a Dutch girl dancing in wooden shoes. The Block had her absolutely stopped.

Afterward, tucking her things into the basket of her bicycle, she gazed down the street, past small dark trees and a white steeple, toward the wet green meadows. Am I going to be like Christi? She wondered. Telling myself, two years from now, that I was better then?

The Cold Draft

Sissy came shivering from her sleep. She had been hearing the hot, ringing shriek of her father's power saw ripping through a sheet of plywood, and had tasted the smoky aroma of sawdust rising through the intricate system of drafts in the old hotel. As a carpenter's daughter, she knew the blade would have to be sharpened soon, for the dulled teeth were burning the wood. And she heard, very faintly, the moaning in the wall, like the cries of a prisoner in a dungeon, and the rustle of what she hoped wasn't a rat.

All this information trickled through her mind, but then the noise and fragrance ceased and new thoughts stole in.

He's gone out for something. Since I didn't hear the pickup, he isn't going far. He'll leave a note on the counter. It's late. I heard a logging truck backfiring down the Wildcat Grade, and now it's going under my window, so it's at least nine.

She opened her eyes, yawned, and gazed out the window. Her bed was tucked into a bay window of her room, that actually bulged a couple of feet into the intersection of Main and Redwood streets. If the floor ever gave way, she would drop fifteen feet to the sidewalk. The sky was gray and had the texture of sand ripples. A hat rack of a small-town telephone pole was etched against it, cobwebbed with wires. A chilly wind blew on her face.

She threw back the covers, pulled on fluffy blue slippers and a robe, and went to the bathroom. Downstairs, she found a message on a scrap of plywood on the hotel desk.

Sis:
Gone to bank to pick up three $1,000 bills!
Then to H's office to pay off the gorilla he calls his manager.
Andrea called.

Sissy trotted back upstairs to dress. She pulled on a long-sleeved green leotard, jeans, and red tennis shoes. Faintly, the bell on the counter tinkled like ice cubes in a glass. "Andrea?" she cried opening the door.

"Hi! I'm doing some shopping for Mom. Want to come along?"

Sissy went backward down the stairs, for practice in knowing where her feet were at all times. Andrea was doing a handstand by the counter. "Can you wait while I eat?" Sissy asked. "I've got to shop too."

"Okay. Whose picture is on the thousand-dollar bill?"

So Sissy knew she had read the note. "I don't know." Andrea followed her into the big hotel kitchen. "Some politician's, I guess."

"Why not a gymnast's some time?" Andrea said. "Who would you write to about it?"

"Hey, neat! A girl in a leotard, and a famous gym on the back! A pink ten-dollar bill!" Giggling, she peered into the refrigerator.

"Not a 10 — a 9.75!" Andrea cried. "Ten's the ultimate score!"

Sissy formed a wheel of ground meat and started it frying. On a tray, she placed a dish of applesauce, a glass of milk, and a plate. Andrea watched her drop a slice of brown bread in the toaster.

"You eat like a horse and don't get fat," she complained. "And I look at a fudge ad and gain two pounds."

"It's not the fudge you *look* at that does it. A school nurse gave me an emergency course in nutrition. I'd started falling asleep in class about ten o'clock, and finally the teacher asked me what I'd had for break-fast. I told her — a chocolate breakfast-bar. So she sent me to the nurse with my lunch box. I had a cupcake, a piece of candy, and some cookies that day."

"What'd the nurse say?"

"She dumped it all in the wastebasket! Then she got a meatloaf sandwich out of her little refrigerator and made me sit down and eat it. It was her own lunch. She told me I'd get soft bones, lose my hair and teeth, and probably go crazy on that kind of diet. I felt like an old woman when she let me go. And she sent a note home to my mother and checked my lunch box every day for a week."

The toast popped up. "You mean your *mother* gave you a lunch like that?"

"Mom majored in cheerleading," Sissy

said. "All the fast-food delivery men knew me by my first name." She deepened her voice. " 'Hi, Sissy, here's your pizza. Your mother's at ballet rehearsal. That'll be a dollar forty-nine.' — Drag a mat into the dining room and practice splits while I eat," she said.

The high-ceilinged room was littered with antiqued furniture; on a small clearing near the windows rested a flowered rug, and upon it there was a round oak table. Beds, chairs, and dressers from rooms being renovated had been stored under white sheets. Sissy always took a chair facing the windows so that she could watch the passing traffic — what there was of it. Andrea groaned as she stretched her stubby legs into the first split of the day.

"You've got to take the pain today to do the trick tomorrow," Sissy said, piously. "That's what Bonnie says. I wonder why she picked Meadowdale instead of some bigger town to open a gym?" she said, chewing a bite of toast.

"She grew up here. She was with a dance group in the East, on television programs, and then her grandfather died and left her the church. It was perfect for a gym. I guess she wanted to come home anyway. She sure asked for it, though!"

Sissy looked at her. Andrea's tone implied that Bonnie was on her deathbed. "Oh — ! you mean Ruby?"

"Yes — Mrs. Bad News herself. Ruby will do anything to beat us in this meet. I'll bet they wipe us out, too."

Sissy laughed. "Hey, cut it out! With that attitude, you might as well not show up. Remember, they've got their problems, too."

"But there's seventy Raskells, and only about twenty of us!"

"But only twelve from each club can compete. And don't forget — not wishing them any bad luck — but just suppose Juno or one of the Long twins gets sick or breaks a leg?"

They giggled. Then Andrea looked startled. "Or what if one of us does! — There's your father," she said, suddenly.

He passed the windows, striding fast with an envelope in his hand. Sissy said, "Oh, good! good!" He must have paid off Mr. Heinrich, and was bringing the receipt home! They were out of the hot water again.

She heard him cross the lobby, enter the

kitchen, and rattle the blue enamel coffeepot as he lifted it from the little wood stove in the kitchen — the "trashburner," it was called. In a moment he came in. He said, "Hello, ladies," but did not smile. He stepped over Andrea's outstretched left leg and stood across from Sissy, while he put sugar in his coffee. He tossed the envelope he carried onto the table.

"Run your eyeballs over that, my good woman," he said to his daughter.

Sissy clapped her hands together. "Did you pay off Heinrich's gorilla?"

"The office was closed."

Andrea scrambled up as Sissy removed three bills from the envelope. Sissy looked, and gasped. A whole string of zeros! But when she ticked them off with her fingertip, there were only three. "A *thousand-dollar bill!*" squealed Andrea. Sissy turned a bill over and squinted at the intricacy of scrolls, gauzy scarves and numerals, and patriotic phrases streaming gracefully across the bill like an advertisement towed behind an airplane.

"Three thousand dollars!" Sissy chortled.

Sissy's father sipped the coffee, then silently collected the bills. Suddenly Sissy

frowned. Gooseflesh ran up her arms. She
glanced at Andrea, and found she was looking back at her, too.

"Feel that?" Sissy said, awed.

It had felt as though the ancient hotel had
given itself a shake, like a dog.

"Yeah!" Andrea said.

"Feel what?" asked Mr. Benedict.

Sissy raised one finger for silence. But
whatever she had *felt* was more like something *heard*, a bass note so deep it was received better by the stomach than the ears.

"Earthquake?" asked Andrea.

"No. The chandeliers would be swaying."

"I hear it now," said Sissy's father. "Some
kind of heavy equipment on the road. Logging truck, maybe."

Sissy hoped he was right. Wouldn't it be
sad if (after all the hotel's struggles, and
barely being saved from demolition) its
backbone had cracked, and, with a deep
death-rattle, it was quietly sinking into its
grave?

Carrying his coffee mug, her father
headed upstairs, leaving the empty envelope
on the table.

Sissy got a card and a ballpoint, and
made up a shopping list. Then she put the

breakfast things back on the tray with the empty envelope and carried everything to the kitchen. She raised the lid of the small heat-stove and placed the envelope on the gray-red coals. So much for Heinrich! The paper turned brown, curled like bacon, and ended in a brief explosion of yellow flame. Then it was a trembling ash, a mere ghost of paper. So much for Heinrich's gorilla, too!

She heard a truck engine blatting in the street. Andrea ran in. "The biggest darned machine you ever saw!" she gasped.

"Logging truck?"

"No. It looks — well — " Andrea looked everywhere but at Sissy. "It looks like, uh, one of Mr. Heinrich's wreckers. I mean, kind of."

Sissy ran for the front door of the hotel.

Rats in the Wall

Heinrich's main man, as Sissy's father called Mr. Grorty, backed the crane onto the vacant lot across from the hotel, and he and a workman jumped from the cab. Mr. Grorty was tall, spare, and dark, tough and crooked as a snag in a forest, and he did everything tilted forward at a half-run.

Sissy's father came roaring down from his office and out the door. Sissy and Andrea watched as he strode to where Grorty stood.

"What's going on?" he shouted.

Grorty tilted his head to peer up at the skinny framework rising into the sky. "I'm rigging a wrecking ball is what's going on," he said.

"Why here?"

"Ask Haskell Heinrich. I only work for him."

"Not here — you don't work for him here. I was just over at your office with the money, and you were closed."

"Try us again. We're closed for a few days while we bid on demolishing an old bank in Eureka."

"Fine. I'll put it in the mail."

"Suit yourself. But she stays here. Red Ball owns the lot she sets on."

The workman had muscled a red iron wrecking ball into position. On its shining red surface someone had painted a have-a-nice-day face. Grorty climbed up on the flat-bed of the machine and set about fixing an iron hook to the ball.

"In fact," said Sissy's father, "I'll mail it right now, so it will be between Heinrich and the post office department."

"Suit yourself," said Grorty.

Sissy's father seemed determined to pro-voke a scene with Mr. Grorty. He pushed his hard hat back and said, "You don't scare me. If that ball should by *any* accident, in *any* manner — touch *one board* of my hotel, I'll sue Heinrich for all he owns, and take you apart like a dime-store airplane kit."

"Isn't that remarkable," said Grorty, buffing the ball with a greasy rag.

Sissy's father stormed into the hotel.

"Those apes! Those morons!"

Sissy and Andrea were leaving to shop when Sissy remembered that she had no money. She sprinted upstairs: "Daddy?" She looked into the Twain Room, which besides being his bedroom was his office, and saw him seated at the desk, staring blankly at it. He glanced around.

"That's funny!" he said.

Sissy sniffed. The smell of Mr. Grorty's cigar had penetrated all the way up here from the street. "What's funny?"

"I'm sure I left the money right here on the desk. I was getting a deposit slip ready to bank it, so I could send the check. In fact, there's the deposit slip under my cup. But where's the money? Got it! I must have left it in the envelope!"

Sissy's stomach sank like a rock into a lake. "I sure hope you didn't, Daddy."

"Why?"

"Because I put it in the trashburner. It burned up."

He made a grunting sound, as though he had been punched in the stomach, but then shook his head. "No, no, Princess, I'm *positive* I left the bills right here when I went downstairs."

Sissy did a half-pirouette and stared at the

window across the hall. It was open. Through it one could see the dark brick of the adjoining building, across six feet of space. "Maybe they blew through the window — !"

She darted to the window and looked down. Between the two buildings ran a narrow passageway which started at a gate on Main Street and traveled to an alley in the rear. Directly below the window was a rickety platform on which rested a rusty oil barrel, part of an old heating system. A ladder, its rungs clotted with dried paint, rose from the ground to the platform. Her father had started to remove the platform once, but had never finished the job.

She heard him pounding down the stairs and saw him appear from the back door of the hotel. He looked about, poked into the three trash barrels lined up under the platform, and searched all the way to the gate on Main Street. Then he came to the ladder and looked up. He climbed to the platform, reached for the sill, and pulled himself up. Panting a little, he clambered into the hall.

"They didn't go thataway."

"But there are so many drafts in the building, Daddy, that the rooms are like lungs. — Well, if they didn't blow out the window — "

She dropped to her knees and crawled around looking under the furniture. Then she rose, pushing her hands through her hair like a madwoman. All the fears and strong emotions of the last couple of days sank to the bottom of her stomach. She felt as though she had eaten a cannonball. Suddenly she wailed. Her father laughed and caught her in his arms.

"It's only money! We'll find it."

"But what if we don't?" she sobbed. "We're ruined!"

He laughed. "But we *will*! That's the whole point."

"What if somebody climbed the ladder and took it and went back down?"

"Nobody could have known it was here. No, baby, there is some very logical explanation to it all."

That night, lying in bed thinking starkly of their loss, she heard the eerie moaning in the wall once more, and a rustling sound, as though rats were building a nest. She pulled the blanket over her head to muffle the sounds.

The Raskells' Secret Camp

"You're next," Bonnie told Sissy, as she stood with Holly and Patsy Moss near the uneven bars. Sissy walked to the starting position before the lower bar. "Hey! Look alive!" Bonnie said, giving her a pat.

Sissy nodded. She didn't feel alive; she felt numb. Did Bonnie know about the money? She pulled her arms in close, pressed her palms against her thighs, and waited with her chin tucked in. The warmups had tired her. She tried to think through the moves.

Glide . . . stoop-through to support position atop the bar . . . change grip to reverse . . . front seat circle.

"No hitches, now. Keep the flow of movement going."

Out of the corner of her eye, Sissy saw a girl come from the vestibule. She passed through a bluish patch of sunlight on the floor beneath a stained glass window. It was Christi Haddon — two hours late! But Sissy hadn't time to speculate. She gazed intently at a chalk smear on the lower bar. She hunched her shoulders, and finally raised her arms. She rose to her tiptoes, then made the little dive to the lower bar. She glided under it, coming back in a stoop-through with her body arching up between her hands, straightening just in time to lift her onto the bar. She changed to the reverse grip, and went forward in a front seat circle. As she came back to the support position, she reached quickly for the high bar. She heard Bonnie say,

"Keep it going, now!"

She made a long hang kip onto the high bar, let her momentum carry her into a forward hip circle, and then cast up onto the bar with the soles of her feet planted on either side of her hands. She let her weight fall back, swung under the bar fast, and came up at full length parallel to the floor. Catlike, she squirmed over, changing to the overhand grip. She swung down hard, flying forward until the lower bar caught her across the thighs. She wrapped around the bar and circled it backward. Then there was the blind, scary moment of cutting loose from the lower bar and flying backward and up — the eagle catch — when your hands either closed on the bar you could not even see, or they fumbled and you fell.

It was there this time. She heard some girls clapping as her hands closed strongly on the bar. Her momentum carried her back. It was all done so fast, now, that your nerves had to remember, for there was no time to think. Drop to the low bar, kip yourself atop it, and catch the high bar again. Swing across the low bar with your legs in straddle position, and straighten them out across the bar. Then bring them back between your hands on the high bar, in a deep pike, as you worked for the speed to rise above the bar, flying backward and cutting away in a straddle cut dismount. With the last of her strength she left the bar, feeling it whip her back — much too strongly, for she was coming down off balance. She fell on all fours.

But I was pretty good! she thought, in surprise. I was very good!

But Bonnie said nothing, and she looked up in disappointment. "How do you feel about it?" Bonnie asked.

"Pretty good. A little slow?"

"Very. When you start a hip circle, straighten out — extend. Then, as you come up, pike in a little. You'll get more speed. But I did like it!"

Sissy did a little chassé skip as she trotted back to the wall to wait with the others for another turn.

"Christi?" Bonnie called.

Christi was just starting some warmup laps around the room. Sissy saw her halt and look toward Bonnie, her pretty face sulky. She wore her old SCATS leotard, and her fair hair, pulled into a bun, had tight waves like the grain in fiddleback maple.

"How does it look?" asked Bonnie.

"How does what look?"

"The Raskells' camp."

Christi's features reddened. "Uh — okay," she shrugged. "Mom drove me up to see — well — what they've got."

"What *have* they got? Ernie Ware told me they were all going up to gymnastics camp until time for the meet. I'd been wondering why I hadn't see any of them around lately."

Christi traced a design on the floor with her toe, sounding disinterested. "Ruby's rented the old Baptist summer camp at Lake Hoopa. And she's got a new coach, a guy named Ted. They eat meat three times a day, and they can't walk anywhere — they have to run. Gazelle's taken off four pounds."

"Sounds like Navy boot camp," Patsy Moss said.

"Kind of. This guy finally got Gazelle to do a backward handspring on the beam! She showed me. She's really got it."

"On the *beam*? It's not fair," Patsy stated. "It's like they were professional boxers or something, getting ready for a fight."

"Yeah," Christi agreed, nodding. "That's the way they all acted."

The girls agreed it was unfair. "I bet they all turn to zombies!" Holly cried. "They'll do their floor exes in lockstep."

"It's still not fair," Andrea said. "Anybody could lose weight and learn fast. It's like the Russians. Like it's all they do."

Sissy frowned at Bonnie, who was listening quietly. It *was* unfair. Ruby was making an Olympic competition out of it. It was supposed to be fun, and good for you, but it wasn't fun when people practically drafted you into the Army to beat it into your head. On the other hand, what was to keep a girl from practicing a lot, and dieting, and working out anywhere, if she had the determination? In fact, she realized, the camp would make no difference at all, probably, to girls who were willing to work; the difference would be that the girls who weren't sure it was worth the effort would be forced to progress anyway.

"What's their new coach like?" Bonnie asked.

"He's just fantastic! He's sensational on the trampoline. He doesn't joke and kid around either. Shape up or ship out, he tells them. I never saw him smile."

"Bonnie almost went to the Olympics, too," Sissy said. "So what's the difference? And I'll bet he can't dance, and she's danced since she was six years old."

"I'm not arguing!" Christi said. "Bonnie asked what they have, and that's what they have."

"Who's arguing? Anyway," Sissy said, "how many beams can you use at once? And what's keeping us from practicing eight hours a day, if we want? Know what I think? I think Ruby's desperate! She's trying to psych them up."

"Do they yell 'kill!' and 'Geronimo'?" Holly asked.

Bonnie slapped her hands together. "Let's see you kill those unevens, Holly! Christi, get going on your laps."

"Well, you stopped me," Christi mumbled as she jogged off down the wall.

For the rest of the workout there was a subtle but definite difference in the session, Sissy realized. You could almost see a hawk-eyed head judge at her card table, watching for flaws. When Bonnie called, "Push!" or "Stretch!" you could see girls trying to please her. "Learn to use your bodies so you can forget them," she said. "So know where you are at any moment, in any trick."

At five-thirty she turned off a jazz record and the girls slumped. They drifted into the vestibule to pull on their street clothes. But feeling good about themselves, Sissy knew, feeling surer. She was glad Christi had sneaked up to Lake Hoopa.

Butterflies and Caterpillars

Prowling toward the cheval glass in her
father's room, Sissy came from the hall door.
As each foot advanced, the opposite shoulder
pushed forward. "Work with your head.
Look at a spot on the wall — look straight
ahead," she heard Bonnie saying. It was
called an isolation routine. Head and shoulders were not welded to the spine, she told
them — they could move independently.
Head, shoulders, and hips must work indi-
vidually, as though the joints were well-
oiled and loosely connected.

"Think of yourself prowling into a room
— kind of catlike."

The telephone rang and she ran to get it,
plopping into her father's desk chair, reaching for the telephone, and tilting back. It
would be Andrea, wanting to talk about the
Raskell's boot camp.

"Hi, baby," her father's voice said.

How did he know I was on the line? she wondered.

"I'm afraid to ask, Frank, but have you found it?" said Bonnie's voice. Sissy knew she should hang up — the call was for her father — but she wanted to hear. For instance, she hadn't known he called Bonnie "baby."

"Not yet, but I'm thinking positive."

"Where could it *possibly* have gone?"

"Several places. Into the trashburner with the envelope. Sissy burned it."

"Oh, Frank!"

"Outside chance — one in a hundred. I can close my eyes and see that money on the desk, right by the checkbook and deposit slip. I go downstairs to hassle Heinrich's gorilla. I come back and it's gone. Did it blow off? This place is full of drafts, and there was a pretty good breeze this morning. But if it did, where did the bills go? Out the window? Huh-uh. We looked."

"Under the bed? The desk?"

"Sissy crawled around for hours. There's a possibility — I can't really see it happening— of someone's climbing the ladder while we were downstairs, stepping inside, and finding the money. Back in the city — heck,

I'd *expect* it to happen. But I've gotten careless up here."

Then a long pause, and Sissy tried to remember how the envelope had felt. Empty? Or — be brave! — with just a little something in it?

"How much time do you have?"

"It's not due for three weeks, and then it would probably take months to put us out on the sidewalks with our suitcases. But what do I do in the meantime? I can't afford to keep dumping money into a building they're going to — er, scrap, anyway."

"Will you look for a job?"

"I had an offer last week. Foreman on a supermarket complex in Los Angeles. I worked for the guy before. Pretty good money, if you like living in Cement City. They won't start for a month or more. So . . . what about this boot camp of the Raskells?"

Bonnie sighed. "Oh, it's just a gimmick. Great for the girls, really. But how many girls can afford — or *want* — to live under all that stress as a regular thing? Ruby's just trying to wipe me out. Then it'll be back to business as usual. Actually, my girls worked better after they heard the news than they've ever worked! But I suppose it'll wear off."

"What are you going to come up with to block Ruby?"

"Nothing. I'm not fighting a war. I never did want this stupid match."

"But it's your war, now, and you've got to win it."

"Okay, but I'll do it with talented kids who want to work. That's the whole point — each girl is different, and they all keep you guessing. You can't feed them all the same stuff and get the same results. If I treated Holly Webb like I treated Sissy, she'd quit. She's talented, but she isn't willing to work. We call girls like her queen bees — into everything, natural talent, but no taste for the drudgery that makes champions. And Christi — great ability, but zero in girlish grace. She's our best on the bars, but weak on floor exes and the beam, where grace is so important. If I could get her to make *one feminine move*, the whole thing would come together, just like that!"

"And what about my little drudge? How's she coming?"

"Nicely."

"But is she good?"

"Yes! But she can't break through to

something she's reaching for. . . . Spontaneity, I'd call it. Style."

"She looks pretty stylish around here," Sissy's father said. "Every move she makes is spontaneous, from sliding down the banisters to carrying plates of food on the top of her head! Don't knock my kid."

Bonnie laughed.

Then Sissy's father said: "Tell me something. Man to man. What happens if Ruby blows you out of the water next week?"

"I lose a few girls, maybe. And new girls may hesitate about joining. Who wants to join the Meadowdale Losers? Join the Raskells and be a champ. Actually, I worry more about the big four-club invitational meet just before school starts. Because after that, the talking begins, and everybody new in the area picks her club."

"And if the worst happens and you don't have enough girls left to pay the bills?"

"I'll buy some hymnals and turn the gym into a church!"

Sissy waited for the dial tone, then carefully hung up. The meet did matter, though Bonnie wouldn't admit it. If they got demolished, and Ruby advertised it all over the country, the Butterflies might as well turn into caterpillars.

Accident!

Sissy mounted the balance beam as though she had helium in her peds, effortlessly and with elegance. She heard the beam judge applauding, though it was against the rules. Then she went into a breathtaking routine of turns and pivots, leaps, wheels, and rolls, which ended in an instant's hesitation in which she realized that the whole gym — it was the Redwood College Gym, and the steeply tilted bleachers were filled — grew quiet. Everyone was waiting for her aerial walkover. (They had heard about it, and now they were going to see it!) She extended her arms like a bird's wings, fingers spread, took a short step, and started the aerial walkover. She leaned forward and pushed off her front foot, her arms still extended. She saw the beam below her, waiting for her. Tonight the narrow wooden path looked a yard wide. A split second later she felt her foot touch the wood, then the other foot came down exactly on course, and she landed in balance, smiling. The judge clapped again, and wrote 10 on her score card.

The perfect score!

And the perfect dream, she realized, as she opened her eyes in her room above Main Street. For a moment she felt like crying. But — but *was* it a dream? For, despite all the nonsense, her mind retained a feeling of confidence, which was what it was all about. She tried to hold onto it as she scrambled out of bed. It was something about your takeoff, blocking hard with your takeoff foot, and not letting your head drop. You had to go *up*, not forward, that was the secret! And lift *up* with your arms. . . . Everything rising, not diving at the beam.

Her father's door was closed. It was still early. She ran down the stairs to the lobby. She drew some drapes and morning light flowed in. She turned and looked at her practice beam lying on the floor near the counter. Barefoot, she approached it in her pajamas. She stepped up on the strip of mahogany scarcely wider than her foot. She took a couple of steps, chasséd to the end of the beam, made a turn, and pliéd. Ready! She

93

smiled to herself, took the short step, blocked hard, and went up. She felt her body working for her, everything compact, her legs fully extended, and for a moment she seemed to hang in the air and rotate on an axis, head down. Her body wheeled over, her foot came down squarely, then the other — and she laughed in exultation as she finished the trick!

Someone clapped. "Very nice! What was that?"

She turned. Her father stood in the door to the kitchen, holding a cup of coffee. Sissy ran to him and hugged him.

"That was an aerial! A front walkover without hands."

"A first?"

"Well, I've done it lots of times with Kelly hand-spotting for me. But this is the first time by myself."

"Hand-spotting? You'll have to explain that one."

"The coach puts her hand out and gives you a little boost at exactly the right point — makes sure you finish the movement. Kind of lifts you through it."

"How safe is it to do by yourself?"

Sissy squinted. "Not very. You could get busted up a little. But I had this dream just

before I woke up! I really got the feeling —
the timing, everything. I didn't want to wait.
And I did it, didn't I?" She glowed with
pride.

Her father laughed. "Said the young gymnast, just before breaking her neck."

That afternoon she told Kelly what she had
done. She was afraid to tell Bonnie, yet. "I
did an aerial this morning!" she whispered.

Kelly frowned. "Did your father spot for
you?"

"No. I did it by myself! And then I did
four more of them, without a miss. Did you
ever dream — ?"

Kelly smiled. "Yes. I couldn't sleep, the
first time I did a walkover on the beam. Then
later I did an aerial in my sleep. It's funny
how your mind helps you sometimes — when
you aren't afraid. But listen — " Kelly held
her by the arm and leaned down to whisper.

"I'll keep your secret, but don't do it again
without a spotter. Bonnie would ground you
for a month. You could break an ankle!"

It had started as the happiest day of Sissy
Benedict's life. Riding her bike to the gym,
she had inhaled the cool wind, heard "Rhapsody in Blue," her floor-routine music from

a house she passed, and felt her muscles working as she pedaled. What a beautiful day! At the gym, she went through the warmup routine vigorously, and realized other girls were working better too, as they caught some of her own enthusiasm.

She was still not sure what style meant, but she knew she would find out when she did her first floor routine today. She felt that confident!

Ernie Ware showed up in his ridiculous Gay Nineties black suit, derby, and cane, smoking a cigar and wearing his bug-eyed, mirror-lensed glasses. Sissy was awaiting her turn at a corner of the big mat, hopping up and down with impatience. Ware came over to watch as Sissy suddenly stood at attention, along with three girls in the other corners. Kelly was fiddling with the record player. Bonnie walked purposefully from the vaulting horse, where she was instructing Andrea to hit the board *hard*, not like a prim little lady.

"Ernie, we'd rather you didn't smoke," she said. "It's a fire regulation, and besides it smells up the gym."

"Sorry," Ware said, stubbing the cigar out in a chalk bowl on a stand.

"And that is *not* a Roman ashtray, it's a chalk bowl."

"You make me feel like a leper," mourned Ware. "Ruby doesn't worry about other people's bad habits. Maybe that's because she's got some of her own."

"Yeah!" Holly said. "Riding in that bus of hers was like fighting a brush fire. She burns leaves in her lungs."

Ware smiled, said that was pretty good, and wrote something on a fold of newsprint. "The Long girls — you know them?" he said.

"Of course. They're very gifted gymnasts."

"Ruby was pointing out to me that the reason neither of them has any weaknesses is that they're identical twins. What's your opinion?"

"My opinion is that every gymnast has weaknesses."

The music started, so that Sissy couldn't hear the rest of Bonnie's remarks. Along with the girls in the other corners, she was stepping out on the pattern she could almost see painted on the mat. It was when she came to the back handspring that she suddenly realized something: Style was feeling good about yourself! It was as simple as that. Since the steps were all taped in her head, she could let herself enjoy the moves — even show off a little. For, in a quick glimpse, she saw Bonnie point out to Ware something she had just done. She stepped right and went into a front handspring, landing lightly. Like a butterfly! She smiled.

"Stretch!" she heard Bonnie urge Christi. "Give me more hands."

The feeling lasted all the way through to the final dive tinsica, going over on her hands, landing on the right knee, and finishing in the kneeling position with the arms raised like a bird's wings. The music ended. Sissy scampered to her corner. Bonnie met her there and whispered,

"By George, I think you've got it!"

During the entire workout, Sissy kept stealing glances at the balance beams, long and challenging on their spidery legs. The beam routine came last for her, but finally she was seated on the floor at the head of the line while a girl named Julie, an intermediate, rather cautiously did her compulsory, which now looked childishly easy to Sissy.

Oh, boy! Would I like to do an aerial on that beam! she thought. I could do it! Why not? What's the difference whether the beam's on the floor or four feet in the air? It's still four inches wide.

"I've noticed," said Ernie, rather pompously, the instant expert, "that the girls have more trouble doing, say, a walkover on the beam than they do on the mat."

"Oh, and you can't figure out why?"

Ernie had put another cigar in his mouth, but wisely hadn't lighted it. "Psych themselves out, I guess. Same exact width."

"Have you ever been up on a beam, Mr. Ware?"

"You can call me Ernie, Bonnie. No. Don't think so."

"Take off his shoes, girls," Bonnie cried. "Mr. Ware's going to walk the plank."

Six girls held his legs while two others unlaced and pulled off his old-fashioned, knob-toed shoes. He was a good sport about it. A chair was brought and he climbed up, getting chalk dust all over his black pants. "Now I've got chalk every place but on my socks, where I need it," he said. "What am I supposed to do?"

He still wore his derby and carried his cane and was gripping the cigar nervously in his teeth.

"Just walk to the end and jump off."

"Don't look down!" Holly warned.

Ware went one foot at a time, very cautiously and with much swaying from side to side. Halfway down the beam, he groaned, "My *feet* are wider than this rotten thing!" But he kept going, using his cane like a tightrope walker working a balancing pole. At the end, he scrunched himself together as though he were thirty feet above a swimming pool, and jumped. He landed so hard his hat fell off. The girls laughed.

"It's impossible," he said. "Nobody ought to do tricks up there on that thing! It ought to be ruled out."

"I'm glad you appreciate the girls' skill now. — Sissy?"

Right then Sissy knew she was going to Do It.

She thought she could work it in right after the scissors English handstand, when she would be coming down in position for a jump. But instead of an ordinary jump, she would take a step and go into the forward aerial. Yet Bonnie, standing near Ernie Ware, watched every move she made. And then, a few seconds before the handstand, Kelly called to Bonnie and Bonnie turned away.

All *right*! Sissy thought. She hoped Mr. Ware was still watching.

She did the handstand, square on the beam, bringing her legs down into a split, then switched them, held it a moment, and arched down on the left leg. But then she had to make a little hitch, because she was on the wrong foot for the takeoff. She made the adjustment, extended her arms, and blocked — just as Bonnie screamed:

"*Sissy!*" She had turned back and seen, in the snapshot of her gymnast's eye, what was going on.

Sissy froze for a moment, but it was too late to stop, and she was going forward and up, pivoting on the nonexistent axis through her shoulders, high and fast. Then she saw that the beam below her was an oblique line rather than a straight one. She was out of position! In that final gasp of time she tried to twist, but her leading foot came down an inch too far to the left, and her trailing foot missed almost completely. And now she was landing awkwardly on the mat.

She heard a *crack* in her ankle as she sprawled on the mat. The pain was so sharp that she did not even try to break her fall.

Cold Packs and Hot Film

"The crack you heard," the doctor said, "was the joint going back into place. No fracture, young lady. The fall dislocated the bones for an instant, and the ligaments snapped them back. Cold packs — elastic bandage — be all right in a week or two."

Sissy assured Bonnie she would practice other things until the meet — arm exercises, handstands, beam, and bars. "I'll be ready — honest!"

But Bonnie was preoccupied that evening as she searched the hotel refrigerator for something to cook. She had driven Sissy to the doctor and then home. Now Sissy sat in a chair in the kitchen with an ice pack on her ankle, while her father helped Bonnie.

"I'm surprised at you, Sissy," he said. "You had strict orders, didn't you?"

"Yes, but I was feeling so sure of myself — "

"Actually, if *I* hadn't panicked, it wouldn't have happened," Bonnie said. "Is there any ground meat? I saw what she was going to do, and I lost my head. If I'd kept still, she'd have made it. She's never been so sure of herself. Will you drive down and get some meat, Frank? And some buns."

The telephone rang and Sissy picked it up. It was Andrea. Sissy reported what the doctor had said.

"Won't you be able to compete?" Andrea wailed.

"Sure! Anyway, I'll be at the gym tomorrow. It doesn't even hurt when I walk . . . much."

"Now you see there are reasons behind rules," Bonnie lectured Sissy, at dinner.

"But I knew I could do it, and I wanted to show off for Mr. Ware. And you said good gymnasts like to show off. And anyway I'm all right. Really!"

"You're our spark plug, you know," Bonnie said. "When you're up, the other girls are up; when you're down, it's like a funeral."

"If we win the match — and the invitational too — will we get a lot of new girls?" Sissy asked.

"Probably. There are girls from nearby towns, driving to other clubs, who could more easily come here."

"What's this invitational meet?" asked Sissy's father.

"It's given by the Arleta Aerials, at Redwood, every year. They invite three or four other clubs, and it becomes a kind of swap meet. It's just before school starts, and new kids come and shop for a club to join. Naturally they're looking for a winner."

The telephone burred in the kitchen. It was a man, but for Sissy. Mr. Benedict carried her in and she put the receiver to her ear. "Hello?"

It was Mr. Ware. "Just calling to check on The Iron Butterfly," he said. "How's the ankle?"

"Okay."

"You mean *okay*, or like okay six months from now?"

"Okay next Saturday."

"Great. What happened?"

"Well, I just missed my footing. I shouldn't have tried it without asking permission."

"Why didn't you?"

Sissy giggled. "I was afraid they'd say no."

Her father was listening, too, and he frowned as Ernie said, "I heard a rumble about you and your father maybe losing the hotel. Is that correct?"

Her father shook his head, sternly.

"No," she said.

"I had it from a very good source."

"No!"

"Whatever you say. Good luck with the ankle. I'll be there taking pictures of you Saturday night."

"You can't."

"Why not?"

"They don't allow flash cameras at meets because it blinds us."

"Oh. Hmmm. Well, I'll get a pho-tog to fix me up with some hot film. See you Saturday."

The next day Sissy did handstands and splits and worked at bar basics. Under the brown elastic bandage her ankle was swollen and tender. Bonnie had everybody else practicing running — a simple thing which no one did correctly without learning the technique. The girls took turns running diagonally across the mat.

"A lot of people can run fast," Bonnie explained, "but they can't run fast with power. All right, Andrea — twenty steps, no more, no less." Andrea started off. "Arms up!

Don't let them dangle." Then Holly ran. "Elbows up!" They went on to front handsprings and other basic tumbling tricks. With the meet coming up, Bonnie was getting more critical.

"No, no! You're 'punching' when you land. You sound like you're on pogo sticks. You should hardly be able to hear it when you hit the mat. *Lift*, and land softly."

She was not satisfied with their performance, and said suddenly, "Let's go back to cartwheels. Reach out in the direction you're going — the whole body goes together. — No, Patsy, too loose. All of you guys are losing speed because you don't step out. *Feel* the stretch. *Stretch out!* Kelly, show them."

Kelly did a chain of cartwheels down the floor. The difference was clear. Kelly's arms and legs, like spokes, didn't bend or shorten. When the others started again, Sissy got up and tried a couple down the far wall. But two cartwheels were enough; there was a sharp pain like a knife stab in her ankle. She went home early to pack ice around it again.

Four more days.

She could do more at the next workout, but did not dare attempt a handspring; yet without practice she would lose her timing. And now she was worried that when she did work out again, she would have lost that feeling of confidence she had had for one brief workout.

She crawled around the upstairs floors again trying to see where the three pieces of paper could have disappeared to. Then she stood in the hall before the alley window and prayed for the answer. Her father was keeping the window closed and locked these days. She raised the sash and felt the breeze ruffle her hair. She moved into his bedroom and could still feel a strong draft. In her mind something quivered like a bug's feelers. This is the way it was done! an elfin voice said. Listen to me — but when she listened, the voice went off the air.

She stood and chewed a thumbnail.

It would have been easy for someone to climb the ladder, steal the money, and vanish. And there were drifters around town who would do it. But who would know it was there? Someone who'd been coming up the ladder regularly, waiting for a chance? No, because her father often left his money and keys on the desk, visible from the window, and surely something would have been stolen before now. So what had happened to it?

The Last Practice

On Friday they met for their last practice session. "We're going to be sharp today," Bonnie said. "No loafing, no lazy fingers. Because next time will be for real."

Sissy jogged around the gym with the rest of them, keeping up and trying not to flinch. The hurt in her ankle was a steady thing, an ache each time the foot took her full weight, but it did not get any worse. The trick would be to trust the ankle and not flinch.

The first big test came with the vaults — running the full length of the gym and hitting the Reuther board hard, going up and over in a handspring vault. The pain stayed right with her, but she tried to block it out. She did some good, springing vaults, and then went over to the blue mat for the floor exercises.

Kelly set the needle on the record, and as the music started four of the girls set out on their floor patterns. Sissy sailed through the initial poses and steps with confidence — until the first back handspring. Then the pain in her ankle made her gasp. She clenched her teeth and kept going, but the sharp stabs of pain distracted her. Her stag leap was short. She went on, but the lightness and grace had gone out of her. Her sequence of ballet steps was wooden. At the end of the routine, she realized with despair that she was not ready for the meet. She would be a liability, not an asset.

As she drifted toward the parallel bars, head down, Bonnie took her by the arm. "It's hurting, isn't it?"

"A little. I know nothing's going to happen, but it spoils my timing. I'll get better after I'm warmed up."

"If it really hurts, don't force yourself," Bonnie cautioned. "That's when people really get hurt."

"No, I'm all right. The doctor said it's only pain!"

"Well, that's nice to know!" Bonnie laughed. "Okay, go on to the unevens, but don't do your dismount. There's no use tempting fate."

As she awaited her turn, Sissy thought about confidence, how it came and went. One day you told yourself suddenly, with no reason, I can do it! I've got it, now! So, sure enough, you did everything exactly right. It was like magic. But then some trivial thing happened; you missed an easy move, slipped or stumbled — and the mood flashed from green to red like a traffic light.

As she thought about it, ideas came together in her head like triangles and squares: A gymnast's ability was made up of memory and experience. The memory was in her muscles as much as in her mind. And some days the muscles forgot, and made the most ridiculous mistakes. So there would always be good days and bad, and until you made your first move on any day you wouldn't know which kind it would be. But the better you got, and the greater your faith, the more good days there would be and the fewer bad.

She did a strong, smooth bars routine, good enough that she could smile when she finished.

At six o'clock she heard Kelly say to Bonnie, "I've got to leave, Bonnie. I have a date tonight."

Bonnie said in a lowered voice, "What do you think?"

"Pray for strong ankles," Kelly said. "They're all walking on Sissy's!"

Mystery Coach

Two dozen girls dressed in an exercise room off the big gym that they all knew well, half of them because it was the Raskells' own gym, and half of them because they were ex-Raskells. The atmosphere twanged with nervousness. Over near the door to the gym the Raskells were pulling off the clothes they had driven over in, revealing their yellow and white leotards. Juno and Gazelle and a tall girl named Farrell were brushing their hair, trading a brush around. Once Juno grinned at Sissy and fluttered her fingers, then turned her back.

"I like our leotards better than theirs," Andrea whispered to Sissy, who nodded. The Butterflies' wore dark blue, with a chain of colored butterflies around the neck. They had long sleeves, as the rules of competition demanded. The dozen Butterflies were

111

grouped uneasily beneath a bulletin board, like night strollers who thought they had heard a sound in a graveyard. They brushed their hair, pulled on long blue-and-white socks, did handstands against the wall. They conversed in whispers.

A young man in a red exercise suit came from the door to an office. On his jacket were the words, TEXAS STATE. He sported a light brown beard, and the Raskells straightened up and nudged each other as he crossed the room. They looked guilty and uneasy.

He looked curiously at Sissy, and she said, "Hi!" with a smile. She knew it must be the new coach, Ted. He looked her over, shrugged, and went on.

"Well, *big deal!*" Sissy whispered to Holly. "I said hi, and he just shrugged."

They heard Ted say to the Raskells, "What'd I tell you guys about chattering? Huh?"

They shut up.

Through the door, Sissy had been watching Bonnie, Ruby, and a young man with a mustache and tousled blond hair who carried a clipboard. Ruby came into the room, taller and thinner than Bonnie and with a race-horsey build. Her blonde hair was done in a long ponytail, and she had an unlighted cigarette over one ear. Her nose was lanky and she had a quick, dissatisfied stare.

"Okay, girls," she said loudly. "Class I — you'll start at the beam and work counterclockwise around the floor. Class II, the floor exercise. Class III, the vault. As soon as you've finished the vault, your unevens. We're going to keep things moving."

All at once it hit Sissy. The beam first!

"Bonnie — ?" she whispered. She saw from Bonnie's expression that she had just realized the same thing Sissy had: that she was starting on the worst possible event for tricky ankles. If she fell, she might be crippled for all the other events.

Bonnie said, "What about splitting some of the girls off to the horse, to take traffic off the — the other — ?" It sounded unconvincing, and Ruby's thin, unpainted lips smiled. She looked like a policewoman making an arrest. It was clear to Sissy that she had planned it ever since someone told her about Sissy's ankle.

"Too complicated, don't you think, Ted?" she said.

"Don't make a bit of difference that I can see," Ted said. "Let's get this show on the road. Be here till four A.M."

Bonnie sighed and accepted it. "Girls,"

113

she said, "we'll line up here and go in to that jazz march. As you enter, line up down the right, facing the bleachers across the floor. Each team will be introduced as a unit, and all the members will take one step forward. Then we'll go to our individual events."

They lined up, Raskells first, Juno the Number One Raskell. She looked vibrant, strong, and ready for anything. Like all the Raskells, her hair was done in a bun.

The march rattled the loudspeakers. Juno stepped confidently through the door. Sissy heard people applauding. It seemed ten minutes later that she herself reached the gym. It was a large, bare gymnasium. A small audience of parents, kid brothers and sisters, and girls interested in gymnastics had been concentrated near the top of the bleachers. They clapped.

The balance beam was at the left, two judges at card tables near it. The forty-foot, blue floor mat was at the far right, on the near side. Beyond the mat was the leather vaulting horse, at the head of a line of red mats running along the far side of the gym. Between these mats and the beam were the parallel bars.

Below the bleachers were tables for the

head judge and an assistant. At each piece of equipment stood another card table where a judge sat with her score sheets. Small girls who were not competing would serve as runners between the judges and the head judge.

An official made some announcements about the order of events and the scoring. Glancing down the line of Butterflies, Sissy saw the girls' clenched jaws, the nervous fingers adjusting clothing. The Raskells stood at attention. They looked sharp, Sissy had to concede. Ted had scared them into conformity; had he taught them anything else?

"Will the judges take their places?"

Andrea looked at Sissy, pale and nervous. "Where do I *go*?" she whispered urgently.

"Floor ex! Class II."

Andrea scampered off to the far end of the gym. As Sissy was hurrying to the beam, at her left, a man in a pink shirt blocked her way. He wore black pants, striped suspenders, and tennis shoes, as a concession to the rules about street shoes on the polished hardwood floor.

"How you doing, Tiger?" he said. It was Ernie Ware.

"Okay! I have to hurry."

"How's the ankle?"

"Pretty good. Fine." She could see herself in his mirror shades.

"Going to stomp all over them tonight?"

"We'll try!"

She trotted to where the other three Butterflies were gathered, looking nervous as they waited for her. Only Holly was making any pretense of warming up. She was doing valdezes, which she wouldn't be using anyway. But at least she did her best in competition. Christi stared gloomily across the floor toward the small crowd of spectators. Patsy Moss was waiting with her arms crossed and her chin jutting out defensively. Sissy recognized the mood. If her first move was good, she'd be spectacular. If it was bad, she'd fly apart.

"Hey, warm up, you guys!" Sissy said.

"Where's Bonnie?" demanded Christi. "She ought to be here."

"She can't be everywhere."

"Well, we're Class I."

"Prove it!"

Sissy did a walkover, then another. There was almost no pain. Her spirits inched up. She turned and did a handstand with some splits. Nearby, Ted was talking to Juno. He looked angry. The other girls in their yellow

116

leotards were going through a suppling routine. They had already warmed up, but this was a last-minute, tension-releasing exercise.

"Look at them. They're really organized," Christi said.

Sissy and Patsy exchanged looks. "Well, we know what we're supposed to be doing, don't we?" Patsy said.

"Your attention, please!" the loudspeakers boomed. "The first contestant in each event will be from the Butterflies Gymnastics Club of Meadowdale. The second gymnast will represent Haskell's Raskells. The following girls will take their name cards to the score keeper — "

Christi picked up her name card and walked to the easel in the middle of the floor. Andrea trotted from the floor mat, and other girls came from the parallel bars and the vault. When a girl's score was being announced, her card would be placed on the easel, and a runner would display the big card bearing a printed score.

"Why me? Why me?" Christi muttered as she came back.

"Relax!" Sissy told her. "You've done this routine a zillion times. Forget the moves and go for elegance."

And Christi started right out by making a run-on mount in which she lost her balance, and had to jump off the opposite side! With a disgusted glare at Sissy, she resumed her starting position, now a half-point in the hole.

Sissy sat on the mat with the other girls and watched in dismay. Christi had totally psyched herself out. The judges' pencils never stopped moving: bent arms, bent knees, insufficient stretch, lack of coordination — deduct .02, .05, .4 — from the possible but almost unheard-of 10 points. She fell twice more and finished with her wendy dismount on the wrong side! Sissy heard her sniffling when she returned.

Farrell went up next for the Raskells. She was small, sober, and assured. Ted spoke to her and she nodded. She saluted, was recognized and addressed the beam again. After a clean mount, she rose in an arabesque, did a run into a split leap high above the beam, descended, and without a break executed some turns and a lunge. Sissy watched her gloomily. Still, the beam judge was making a few marks on her card, and she nursed a hope that Farrell lacked that mysterious quality called style. For with all her precision, Farrell was a little too solemn and slow.

Now they were calling Holly's name. A runner trotted from the head judge's table with the big roto-index of scores. Christi's name was placed on the easel. The runner turned slowly, letting everyone read the big black numerals. Sissy did not even want to know. To make sure no one missed it, the news also came over the speakers.

"Christi Haddon, Butterflies, 5.7."

Christi received it stonily. In the last spring meet, she had scored over 8 in one try at the beam.

Winners and Losers

We're not licked yet, Sissy told herself. But the scores going up were discouraging. Holly scored 7.8, while Liz Long, blonde and fired-up, beat her with a 9.1! Then they called Patsy Moss, all pep and smiles, who charmed the judges out of their socks. She was in her competition mood tonight, bright and confident. Right from her mount, she showed elegance and zest. And then, at the very last second, she overextended, lost her balance, and spoiled her dismount.

Juno went next, bouncing to her feet and heading for the starting position. But she paused to put her hand on Sissy's shoulder and ask, with spurious sympathy: "Is your ankle okay now?"

Sissy said: "Sure. Fit as ten points."

"Plus or minus?" Juno giggled.

Sissy wrinkled her nose at her.

Harry knelt near the beam to get pictures of his sister. Juno ran on and up with strength. She was almost dwarfish in build, but this compactness was a gymnast's best friend. She did a sharp routine that to Sissy's critical eye was almost military. The moves were programmed into her. Harry snapped several pictures without flash. If Juno had a weakness, it was in being so sure of herself that she hurried the moves. She cartwheeled onto her right arm, made a quarter-turn, dropped to the mat, and raised her arm like the champion of the world.

The spectators cheered.

A runner carried her scores to the head judge, and Sissy wondered how much they had docked her for choppiness and lack of elegance. Maybe I'm catty, she thought. She heard more scores announced. Andrea had made only a 6.5 in her floor exercise because she forgot a move. The Butterflies were demoralized. As if that weren't enough, Gazelle scored an 8.9 for the Raskells.

"Sissy Benedict, Butterflies!"

Bonnie whispered, as Sissy got up from the mat: "Remember! 'I'm the best.'"

Sissy trotted out and saluted the judges. She got a nod and squared off to the beam.

She pressed her palms against her thighs, thinking, You're as good as you think you are — and I think I'm good. I'll show them! She rolled her shoulders once, then rose on her toes, lifted her arms, and ran for the Reuther board. She went up and on, squatting an instant in the completion of her mount. It was perfect. She rose with a smile to an arabesque on her right leg, her left leg stretching back. But as she brought her arms down to her sides, a move at her left distracted her: It was Harry, getting set for a picture!

I will not think about Harry, she told herself, even as she thought about Harry. It's between me and the beam. It's as wide as it ever was, and I know every move of the routine perfectly.

Then there was a scalding flash. The beam, Harry, and the judges were engulfed in purple light. As her vision cleared, she realized Harry had fired a flashbulb. She brought her arms upward, swaying, but had to look down to find the beam.

I'll kill that kid! she thought, in rage.

Bonnie's voice protested angrily.

Sissy kept moving. Three running steps to a leap. She made the leap, but missed her footing. She had the presence of mind to turn, take the fall and land squarely. There was a scuffle, and Harry saying,

"Whattayuh doing! Whattayuh doing? That's a four-hundred-dollar camera!"

Something clattered in the stands. Trotting back, her vision clearing, Sissy saw that Bonnie had yanked the camera from the military school general and hurled it into the empty bleachers. Bonnie went to the judge and protested, and the judge nodded.

"Start over. No penalty," Bonnie told her, hurrying up.

The head judge announced that cameras with flash were not permitted, and please observe this rule. A runner brought out Juno's score: 8.9. Her teammates clapped, and Juno hugged Ted.

Sissy saw the rectangular end of the beam in the heart of a purple blossom. No penalty except on me! The creepy little military-school freak! She tried to hum "Windmills," took a couple of extra breaths, realized she was breathing too fast, and dropped her arms. Then, steadying, she raised them again. She hit the board with a crash and mounted neatly.

Harry was still there, cocking and firing

a thumb. *Pow! Pow!* She ignored him and went into her routine. She made her jumps with sureness, but was suddenly aware that her head was tipped down and she was watching the beam! Lost points. . . . A few moments later, as her ped squeaked in a half-turn squat, she caught herself doing it again. I will not look down! she vowed, and she kept her promise even when she swayed off balance on a simple little skipping chassé. She turned and made a jump to the mat rather than a fall, faced the beam, made a scissor mount, and went on.

She did the handstand, quarter-turn, and dismount, and raised her arm, her right hand resting on the beam. The spectators applauded. But they weren't judges; they didn't have the score cards and pencils. The runner darted away with her score.

When she turned, she saw her father standing behind Harry, talking deadpan to him, and Harry said something jeeringly and marched away. Her father spoke to Bonnie, and then grimly went back to the stands. He spoke to Haskell Heinrich. But by this time Sissy was watching Lori Long, Liz's gifted twin sister, turn in another star performance. Two for the price of one, she thought moodily. Anything Liz can do, Lori can do better.

They moved to the blue floor mat.

More scores were posted: Dana Garvey for the Raskells: 8.6. Vicki Longacre: 7.9, Butterflies. Sandy Pierce: 7.5 for the Raskells. It was clear that the gap between the clubs was widening. Bonnie told the girls:

"Don't look so gloomy! Think of it as a workout with a few spectators. Relax."

Then they announced Sissy's score for the beam exercise, and they all groaned: 6.8. The gap was growing every time the loudspeaker crackled.

Liz Long trotted to her starting position on the mat, and waited for the music. She was smiling confidently when she started. Sissy knew they were going to see something. Liz rode the success wave all the way, her moves full of zest. Yet as she finished, to the applause of the audience, Sissy knew she had done just as well in practice, when everything was working and her ankle was sound.

She took her place, saluted, and waited for the music. She stepped out, pliéd, made a nice tuck jump and a back handspring, and finished the starting sequence with a step-out move. Then there was a movement beside the mat, a glint of chrome, and she flinched as she saw someone with a camera. But it was only Mr. Ware, and he took his picture without a flash. She went on, smiling without conviction, for the flow of movement had been broken. She was behind the music. But in trying to catch up, she moved too quickly, and then in slowing down she overdid it and got behind. At last she came to the dive tinsica, wheeled over to land in balance in the kneeling position, and stretched out her arms.

Bonnie gave her a kiss when she ran off the mat. Pretty good, she knew, despite all her mistakes. When her score was posted, she realized she had done better than she thought: 8.8. Beyond that, the judges were thinking about matters like elegance and style. . . .

It did not take long to wrap it up. Sissy wished she could have done her flashy optional routines. She wished her ankle did not hurt. She wished she could break Harry's camera over his head. For everybody knew they had lost.

". . . Want to thank both clubs for the fine

exhibition of gymnastic work," the official said over the speakers. "Some of you may not realize that there is a specified deduction for each wrong move, even something so slight as a bent finger.

"We've seen a fine show of gymnastic ability, and we can certainly look for champions among these girls who have competed. If you've been keeping score, you already know the winners in this little invitational meet. Overall individual winner among the girls was Juno Heinrich, of Haskell's Raskells, with 34.2 points — !"

Juno raised her stubby arms like a boxer, made a little circle and came back to her teammates.

"While the winners, with 350.8 points, were the Raskells!"

Sissy gazed down the line of teammates and saw Bonnie clapping politely, but not for long. Christi walked off and disassociated herself from the proceedings.

The Raskells swarmed over to commiserate with their victims. "You were really good!" "We were just lucky!" "Juno was *so* good, and when she's up — "

"Liz and Lori," Bonnie was saying, "don't you have *any* weaknesses?"

The pretty, blonde Long sisters looked at each other and said, Well, they were lucky.

"Yeah, you were lucky I sprained my ankle and Harry popped a flash in my face," Sissy said, and walked off.

That tore the camaraderie, and the meet ended in honest bad feeling. Ruby gave Bonnie a leer of her pale thin lips.

"See you in two weeks," she said.

"With optionals and no flashbulbs," said Bonnie.

How to Lose a Meet

Two days after the meet, the Butterflies gathered again in the church. Kelly led the warmups, yelling for enthusiasm. But the girls were as limp as noodles. There was no sign of Bonnie, and Sissy decided she had left town in disgust.

"You look like they were giving a funeral here!" Kelly pleaded. "Come on — stretch out!"

But no one stretched, no one did a real pushup or a vault that did not look like a collapse. Then Bonnie came from her office, and everyone stopped in her tracks. Bonnie was wearing tight, cut-off jeans and a red tee shirt, with red yarn in her braids. She smacked a clipboard against her leg as she looked at them.

"Everybody on the blue mat, and sit down!"

The girls scampered to their places. Sissy felt a healthy tension beginning to pull them together. They were going to get roasted, and were glad of it.

"Anybody dying?" Bonnie asked. "Anybody have to have a doctor after we got whipped? That's good. Because now we've got it out of our systems. We lost big, but we all lived to tell the tale. We know that losing isn't fatal.

"I could give you a list of wrong moves you made that would read like a computer printout. But it wouldn't help, because what was wrong was that we went there determined to lose, and nobody was going to stop us. You were all trying to walk on Sissy's bad ankle, to begin with. Sissy wins us points when she's up. But this isn't a one-girl club. Any girl can be as high as a kite on any night, and any girl can be totally out of it. It's up to *you*, not somebody else. A winning club is one where each girl keeps right on competing. So she falls off the beam — that's only a half-point. She makes a dismount; she can still make all the other moves perfectly."

Holly raised her arm, but Bonnie shook her head. "We'll have questions later. We've got two weeks to get our heads together, and if we don't, then it just means one thing: You've got the wrong coach."

"No! It was Harry!" Andrea cried.

"Harry spoiled Sissy's beam effort, but we did the rest. From now on, I don't want anybody coming to me saying that she won't be very good today because somebody else has a sore shoulder. This isn't a football team: What happens to Holly or Sissy has no effect on Andrea or Vicki. Gymnastics is all individual effort. Christi doesn't realize that, evidently," she added. "She's gone back to the Raskells."

The girls looked at each other and began whispering.

"She's discouraged. I guess I don't really blame her. She's just not able to loosen up and express herself. Some people never do learn. Okay! Forget Saturday night. It never happened. We're starting clean!"

A cool ocean breeze blew through the windows. The taste of it picked Sissy up. They *were* starting clean — they had 10 bright new points apiece for every event, and they were as good as anybody.

"The Redwood Invitational is a fun meet," Bonnie went on. "Four clubs — the Raskells, the Trinity Pirouettes, the Arleta Aerials, and US!"

"Yay Butterflies!" Kelly cried.

"Yay!" the girls yelled.

"The Trinitys and Aerials have some standout gymnasts, but I think we've got more depth. Juno and the Long girls are our real competition. The way we're going to beat them is not to make mistakes. There's no reason you shouldn't do well on your compulsories, so we'll concentrate on the optionals. If there's a trick you aren't comfortable with, tell me, and we'll substitute something else.

"Any questions?"

Andrea raised her hand. "Is Ted teaching them a lot of tricks? I mean, shortcuts and things — ?"

Bonnie smiled. "You dreamer! There aren't any shortcuts. Gymnastics is practice and inspiration. By the way, did you notice how the girls tightened up when he talked to them?"

Yes. They had! Juno liked him, but it had seemed to Sissy that some of the other girls were uneasy with him.

"So who knows?" Bonnie said. "Maybe if one of the girls he's counting on lets him down, he'll lower the boom and scare them all into mistakes. I mean, if you want to dream about revenge, that's one way it could happen! Let's go!"

Muscle Freak

In the late dusk she pedaled her bicycle home. A fine, cold mist swirled down from the wooded hills. She was tired, but with the good weariness that came from working well. She loved the optional routines that Bonnie and Kelly had worked out with her months ago. (Do you like those jazz steps? We'll put in some more of them. And that gainer dismount from the beam — we'll keep that, it's showy.)

Yet, like a mosquito buzzing in her ear, worry about the Block kept pestering her. Merely polishing her routines was not progress. It was like cleaning an old car: It was the same car when you finished. She was like Christi, unable to break through to something new. The little movements of hand, wrist, arm, and finger — she did them too mechanically.

When she left, Bonnie had given her a slip

of paper folded into a square. "Open it when you get home," she said.

At the hotel, she rolled her bike into the lobby and sniffed. Her father had meat cooking. She was starved. "Hi!" she called. She heard him reply from one of the rooms he was renovating. She groped in her windbreaker pocket for the slip of paper and unfolded it. There was only one word on it.

STYLE! Bonnie had printed, in capitals.

Sissy leaned against the doorjamb. Her mouth drew down. Now she was not happy-tired; she was just tired. She closed her eyes and struggled to remember the dream she had had. Style was what the dream had been about; but style was not a move that could be taught, for it was you. It was what you thought about yourself and how you expressed yourself.

She went wearily upstairs and filled the bathtub. Her muscles ached. Lying in the hot water, she thought about the isolation routine they sometimes did. There were some moves in that routine that she felt stylish about — the catlike prowl, the way her shoulders moved independently of her spine. She made a plan: She would do the isolation routine before the big mirror, then kind of slide into her floor-ex routine, and maybe —

maybe she would get the dream-feeling again.

Maybe.

She dressed in an old tee shirt and jeans and her peds, and dug out a half-sheet of paper with her floor-exercise diagram on it. It looked like a problem in geometry, with notes in Bonnie's neat printing. She carried it down the hall to her father's room and placed it on the corner of his desk. *Jazz to corner*, the notes read. *Roundoff, handspring, full-twist*. And so on. She tried some pike lunges and stag jumps to the side, watching herself in the mirror.

"Soup's on!" her father's voice came up the stairs.

She ran down the hall, backed down the stairs, posing as she went. In the dining room, she gave a wail. "Daddy!" Her plate was piled with half the starch in Meadowdale! "Potatoes *and* spaghetti? What are you trying to do to me?"

"That's fuel. You burn up ten million calories every time you practice."

"That's *fat*, Daddy. And I put on nearly a pound last week."

"Naturally. You're growing."

She made a dividing line between what she would eat and what she would not eat.

"Yeah, growing an inch a year," she said. "By the time I'm eighteen, I'll be five-one and weigh two hundred pounds. I'll be *spherical*."

He laughed. "Don't worry, Princess. You'll grow."

"Who wants to be big? I want to be an Elite."

Afterward, she washed the dishes, then went upstairs and faced herself again in the cheval glass. Sissy Benedict — Butterflies Gymnastics Club. Famous for style. The Iron Butterfly. She rehearsed the moves — a leap to a split, then pop up to a pose. But, *hmm*, what came after that? She moved to the desk and glanced at the diagram. Wait a minute. Those are the balance beam notes. She shuffled the papers. I know I left it on top, under the slip that says, STYLE. Where was that one, in fact? And where *was* the darned floor-ex diagram?

She went out in the hall and looked on the floor. But she was sure she'd left it on the desk. In the mirror, as she walked back to the desk, she saw her blank expression, and heard a buzzing like a doorbell between her ears.

They were gone. Gone, like the thousand-dollar bills!

Her father came up when she yelled. They searched methodically.

"The window was open?"

"Yes. But the ladder isn't there any more, because you moved it after — after the last time."

"Was it important?"

"No. I can write it down again. But it might tell us where the bills went if we could find the diagram."

"Okay, now, let's turn on our brains. Full power. Get a flashlight and go over the alley, while I move some furniture — "

Sissy ran downstairs and searched the narrow lane that ran from back alley to street gate. She opened the gate and stepped out onto Main Street. A quiet traffic moved along the street, an after-dinner clearing away of townspeople moving toward television, books, and bed. It did not look like a night when anyone would be out stealing gymnastics routines.

But someone had been.

She closed the gate and went back. Later, in bed, she heard the sighing in the walls, and shivered.

During warmups next day, she worked on

her vault. It was a half-turn on, half-turn off handspring, worth 10 points if perfectly executed. Kelly stood near the horse, calling to her:

"Not too long and low. You'll make bad turns and have to take steps after you land. No steps or hops."

She nodded. Her worst fault was not running hard enough. She pranced down the mat, had a good flight onto the horse, making a half-twist on and landing at the proper angle. But she was late in getting off. She completed the half-twist off, landing with her arms raised, but had to take an extra hop to keep from falling forward.

Bonnie sent her to the unevens. She walked there slowly, trying to get the feel of her new half-turn mount. She hadn't even told Bonnie about it. *Dive for the low bar, twist over beneath the bar before grasping it, rise up on top in a kip.* All bar and beam routines started with a mount and ended with a dismount. High scores called for superior-difficulty mounts and dismounts. She'd practiced this half-turn kip mount at the hotel, since it wasn't dangerous, and now she told Bonnie:

"I can do it, Bonnie. I'll need the points."

"You don't need to lose points by over-reaching. But let's see what you've got."

When her turn came, she placed her hands in the chalk box, thinking soberly.

Standing a few feet before the low bar, she rubbed her hands together. She dropped her arms, gathered herself, and dived flat, twisting upside down. Her hands caught solidly and she kipped up onto the bar.

"Well, well!" Bonnie said. "How about the rest? Just the somi through the drop kip catch, now."

She gathered speed in the front hip circle around the bar, and let herself fly upward toward the high bar in a somersault. From the high bar, she made a drop kip catch and back to the bar. Everything was working.

"And then what — ?"

"Straddle over kip, and a front hip circle, then a cast to a handstand."

"Do it."

She crossed one hand over the other in a pirouette, balanced a moment, and let herself swing down to the bar and around it in the whipping action that ended with her body sailing back, hard and high, onto the high bar in an uprise. From the high bar she soared back and up in a showy hecht dismount.

She landed solidly, a little dazed. She saw Kelly grinning at her.

"You're turning into a muscle freak," she said. "That's why it's going better. You're getting stronger."

She ducked under the bars and went back to the end of the line. "Hey, good!" Holly told her. "Your uprise looked *so easy*."

"It's the strength exercises. It really is," Sissy said, with a warm feeling for the strength circuit.

Later she did the complete routine. Twice she fell, but the sureness would come — the solid grip when you went from low bar to high and back again, the whack against your palm. But it would have to come fast, with less than two weeks to practice.

Christi came by one day and watched a few minutes, looking defiant. "I left some clothes here," she told Bonnie.

"They're in my office. Is it going better?"

"I think so. This guy Ted is so tough! He works us till we drop."

Sissy and some other girls joined them. "Do you like him?"

"Mm — yeah. But you don't have to like a person to learn something from them." She sounded defensive.

"That's true. Raise your right arm."

"What?"

Bonnie raised her own right arm above her head. Christi looked defiant, but raised her arm overhead.

"Now lower it. . . . When you raise or lower your arm," Bonnie said, "pretend you're doing it against a force. You have to *force* it upward or downward, and your hand turns back from the force, like the tip of a bird's wing."

"Yeah, you said that before. I just don't get it."

"But it's still true. How are the Long girls coming?"

"Fine. It's funny how good Lori is on the beam, but on the unevens she's less sure of herself. In a meet, though, she gets all psyched up and does well in everything. They're both that way. Ruby says they're good competers. They get real high for a match."

"They certainly do. And yet there's something odd about them . . ." Bonnie said.

"What?"

"I don't know. I haven't figured it out. Okay, girls. Back to work."

The Beasts from
Haskell's Gym

Up in the mountains Haskell's Raskells were rumored to be turning into snarling, meat-eating, cadence-shouting beasts who would attempt anything. On two occasions, Ernie Ware brought scary reports from the woods and reported the gymnasts' prowess in the paper. Holly went up once to visit her friend Gazelle, and came back in a panic.

"They've all got the most *fantastic* optional routines that Ted cooked up!" she reported.

"Don't tell us about their strengths," Bonnie said with a sigh. "Tell us about their weaknesses."

"Well — it kinda seemed to me they were right on the point of missing a catch or a leap all the time, because so many of the tricks are new. And they don't have much elegance. But I s'pose they will have in competition."

Yet the news kept souring, like spoiled milk. The Butterflies were outnumbered and the Raskells allegedly were developing a horde of supergymnasts. According to the rules, six girls could compete in each event; the Raskells could field four top-rated starters and others nearly as skilled. The Butterflies had to look under the mats to find six girls in any class.

Big guys versus little guy.

The day before the meet, Bonnie asked for a vote on all doing their hair the same way — parted in the middle and combed to little brushes at the side. Their hair would look neat and uniform and not cause point-losses by girls brushing it out of their eyes.

They voted yes on hair.

"I want you all to suit up tomorrow night, in case of last-minute substitutions," Bonnie said. "But we'll start with these six girls in Class I: Holly, Patsy, Debbie, Donna, Tammy, and Sissy." Then she named the Class II and III girls and added:

"We'll work out tomorrow morning. Do your hair late in the afternoon, and be sure you lay out your long sleeves. Don't eat much dinner. I can take three girls in my car, Sissy's father and Holly's can each take three, and I hope the rest of you can work out car pools. Call me if there's a problem.

"Now don't get uptight about winning. Just think about elegance."

"Bonnie?" Andrea cried, raising her arm. "A guy told me they're going to use dirty tricks! He said they're going to set off a firecracker, for one thing."

Bonnie laughed. "The legend of Haskell's Raskells! One dirty trick and the whole team will be disqualified. Don't worry about them, worry about you. If you really concentrate, you won't even think of the audience."

"But the judges — !" Patsy wailed.

"Charm them. A nice smile and a salute. But don't overdo it like Juno. Syrup's going to drip from her mouth."

While Sissy practiced in the lobby that evening, she heard her father talking on the telephone. He called the other man Arnold. Arnold seemed to be a lawyer. Once Mr. Benedict sighed, "Oh, yeah, the hotel will go down like a card house. Heinrich's first toy was probably a sledgehammer. Yes, it is a pity. Okay, Arnold, just thought I'd double check."

After he hung up, he glumly drank coffee for a half hour.

Sissy took a warm bath. She sipped a cup of hot cocoa at bedtime. In bed, she invited dreams. She had a vivid dream-life and hoped that one of her dreams would explain elegance to her.

Once she woke up, but the dream she left was of thousand-dollar bills spinning in a whirlwind down Main Street, and herself being unable to catch any of them. She slept again. And then, very late — it must have been almost morning — a young woman came to her. A woman or a girl. She took Sissy by the shoulders and said to her:

"Do you know me?"

"Of course!"

"I want to tell you three things. You already know them, but you don't realize it. Are you ready?"

The things were simple, but when she awoke they were gone, retreating like wavelets running back to the sea. She squeezed her eyes closed and prayed for the dream to come again.

Something about a lake!

Something about money!

Something about Liz (or was it Lori?).

She strained to see the face of the person who had appeared in her dream, but it had faded too. She cried a little and then got up.

***

BEAT THE BUTTERFLIES!

Sissy saw the motto painted on the red wrecking ball across the street, as she wheeled her bike from the hotel. She parked angrily, went back for a can of spray paint, and fiercely blacked out the words. Harry, probably! That uniformed creep!

She had expected the final practice session to be like telling ghost stories around a campfire, everyone trotting out her particular worries, but Bonnie and Kelly kept them moving. A healthy excitement began to charge the team. Patsy Moss was kept too busy to tighten up as she always did before a meet, and she worked briskly and without temper tantrums. Holly's lazy fingers and toes were beginning to work a little, as they usually did when she smelled a crowd; and Andrea showed good strength in her casts on the parallel bars. Every girl reacted differently to a meet, but the general feeling was one of expectation.

They could hardly wait to see the gymnastic beasts Ruby and Ted had developed in the woods, like little Frankensteins! They might be fantastic in the gym, but how about in competition?

Bonnie spoke to them after practice.

"It's going to be fun, and instructive. Watch the tall girl named Debbie, on the Trinity Pirouettes team. She's a little older, almost a senior, and probably the best in the country. And Vicky Dryer, in the aerials, will show us something on the beam. You can learn from them both."

She handed out little snippets of blue yarn, just the color of their competition leotards, to tie their hair with. And she told them again to eat like sparrows, and to be there on time.

Now it was up to them.

Windup Gymnast

The big gym was arranged as it had been two weeks ago, the equipment gleaming on the polished hardwood floor with its vivid basketball court markings. It looked like a four-ring circus as the teams warmed up on each piece of equipment before a whistle blew and they rotated to the next.

Sissy had a shivery feeling. The hall was chilly, with a subdued babble from the crowd of parents and friends, brothers and sisters, along with people who had never seen a gymnastic meet before but whose interest had been provoked by Ernie Ware's articles in the newspaper. Girls trotted about, bright as tropical birds. Jazz music accompanied a girl from the Trinity Pirouettes as she did a catchy floor routine. Slippers squeaked on the beam. Girls were jumping up and down to loosen their leg muscles, arching from presses into handstands, giving each other back rubs. Ted leveled an arm at his girls, who were whispering as they waited for the vault. They shushed. Sissy and Tammy looked at each other.

"They've turned into zombies!" Sissy said.

The Butterflies moved on to the horse vault. Sissy had just seen Juno do a quarter-turn handspring onto the horse, a three-quarter-turn off. It was a 10-point-difficulty trick. It seemed to her that most of the Class I Raskells were doing very flashy tricks, technically worth the same as less showy ones, but certain to impress the judges — if properly executed.

Bonnie was whispering to Kelly. "Did you notice Juno on the bars? Every time she finishes a move, she glances at Ted for approval! I hope she does it when we get started. She'll lose points."

Someone at the head judge's stand explained how the competition would be conducted. There was nothing new, except that of the six girls who competed in each class, only five scores would be counted.

Then there *was* something new, that caused all the gymnasts except the Raskells to gasp, and then ask questions of their coaches.

There would be no compulsory routines!

It was a time-saving measure, the announcer said. With all the girls competing, etcetera. The Raskells looked smug.

"I could strangle that woman!" Bonnie said. "Why did they let us waste all our time keeping up our compulsories, if we weren't going to use them? But *Ruby* knew! *They* didn't waste time! Darn!"

"Judges, take your posts," the announcer finished.

The music and the slap-thud-thud of the springboard died. Teams gathered near their starting places. The Butterflies were at the balance beam, with the Raskells one position behind them, on the bars.

"Sissy, you're first," Bonnie announced. "Get us off to a good start!" Sissy picked up her big name card and trotted to the official in the middle of the floor.

She went back, checked the height of the beam, and asked them to lower it. Shivering, she placed the Reuther board at one side of the beam end, then took her place. She trembled as she pressed her palms against her thighs, peering at the beam. It looked so narrow! She heard the music start for an Aerial's floor routine.

She tried to salute, but suddenly realized she was not ready! She bit her lip and glanced almost in appeal toward the head beam-judge. Is this your salute? the woman's expression asked. No, it's just terror! I'm not ready. The Block! Why can't I remember the lady in my dream? She'd tell me how to start.

Bonnie caught her eye with a frantic gesture. Coaches were not allowed to give advice at this point, but Sissy knew she was saying: *Just do it, girl!*

She raised her arm and smiled timidly at the judge. *Why* did I have to start with a handstand mount? she mourned. Why not on skates? Something easy?

The judge nodded.

Sissy brought her arm down, took a breath, and ran for the springboard.

She could not loosen up. She knew she was looking down at the beam. Her extensions were cramped, and on her straddle up to a handstand, she almost fell. Doing a front walkover, out, she rose on the narrow catwalk, felt her balance going, gasped, and had to jump off.

Deduct one-half point.

She remounted in despair, did a body wave, posed in a one and one-half turn, and ran into a split leap. Then a perfect up-and-down needle scale, narrow as a splinter, and a lunge. She sank into the side straddle split, her toes curled over the edge of the beam. She pressed to a handstand, then cartwheeled to the end of the beam. Feeling, with every move,

Bonnie was right, I'm a windup gymnast. Why did she send me out first? She knows I'm not up for the meet, that I've got a Block, that I'm clumsy. And they're all worried about me. They won't be any better than I am.

She steadied herself, ran to the end of the beam, jumped high, and went over backward in a perfect gainer dismount. She landed off balance, regained her poise, and stood with a forced smile. Then she dropped her arms to her sides and trotted off. Bonnie hugged her. Sissy tried to smile. But that was one of my *good* events! she thought miserably. What'll I do on the vault and bars?

"Except for that one fall — " Bonnie was saying.

Sissy nodded numbly. She saw one of the Long girls — she had no idea which — run out with her name card, cool, fair, and poised. What had she dreamt about them? Something furtive; something unfair. . . .

"Hey, you looked good out there! My Iron Butterfly." It was Mr. Ware, patting her shoulder. How could he see through those sunglasses? He had nice blue eyes, so why did he hide them?

"Are you going to shellac the beasts from Haskell's gym?"

Hugging herself, Sissy shook her head. "I don't know, Mr. Ware! Please don't bother me. I really have to think."

Ware bent closer. "You think what?"

"I said I — it's *mental*, Mr. Ware! You have to — "

She stopped her desperate muttering and stared at him. From behind the bulging mirrors of his glasses, a girl's face looked out at her. And suddenly she remembered it — the face from her dream! The girl had said — it came clearly, now — she had said,

"I won't desert you, even if everyone else does. I'll always be here."

Ware squeezed her elbow. "Sure, sure — naturally you're a little nervous. It's a big moment, but you're just as big as the challenge. I'll tell you a secret: I've bet ten bucks on you to beat Juno!"

Sissy looked at the Long girl again, then bobbed her head. "I'll try to win for you,

Ernie. But I need something. Do you have an old-fashioned fountain pen? You know, with ink — ?"

Ware pulled a fat orange pen from his coat. "Like this?"

"Yes! May I borrow it?"

"Going to have an autograph party?"

"Sort of. Can you make it squirt?"

"Squirt! Sure, but I wouldn't recommend — "

In his glasses, she could still see the girl who had told her what she herself knew deep in her mind, but could not bring to the surface when she needed help. For there were things you know only in dreams, but sometimes — if you were lucky — you hooked one and landed it like a fish. Just as, in this instant, she had in her hands the three golden fish she had hooked in the dream.

She ran to where the Raskells were clustered near the parallel bars. Ted stood where he could keep his cold eye on Lori Long, who was saluting the judge before starting her mount. The other Long twin sat huddled beside Juno on a mat. Sissy placed herself behind her. She unscrewed the barrel of the pen, as Mr. Ware had showed her, and let the ink drip onto Liz's long yellow sleeve. A blue-black stain took shape. . . .

At first Liz did not realize there was a large pear-shaped blot of ink forming on her right sleeve. She was watching her sister do a catchy routine, marred only by her glancing at Ted as she finished each sequence of it. Then Liz reached up, absent-mindedly, and touched the place where the ink had stained her sleeve. She felt the wetness and frowned at her fingertips, then gasped and scrambled up. She saw the pen in Sissy's hand.

"You dummy!" she hissed. "What do you think you're doing?"

"Oh, gee!" Sissy bit her lip. "Gosh, Liz, I was going to ask for your autograph because you guys are so *good*! Or is it Lori? I never can tell. Is that Lori on the unevens now? Or is it you?"

Liz's face bleached. She looked sick. Suddenly, without a word, she waded through the seated Raskells to Ruby Heinrich's side, whispered desperately, and showed her her sleeve. Ruby stared at the ink blot, then at Sissy. Liz was pleading with her.

"No, of course we don't have extra leotards," Ruby muttered. "It might wash — no, it'd just make a mess. And there's no time — ! Blast that girl!"

Sissy scampered back to her group and sat

155

down with the other girls near the beam, who were watching Holly perform. Only Ware and Bonnie seemed to realize what she had done. Sissy returned the fountain pen to Mr. Ware, who looked puzzled.

"Hey, that was kind of mean, wasn't it?" he said.

"Not as mean as what they've been doing to us. You just watch, Mr. Ware."

Bonnie studied her. Ware went over to the Raskell's group and tried to hear what Ruby was telling Liz, whose name had been called. Sissy sat in a reverie, remembering the dream, trying to fix it in her mind, like a photograph that would fade if it weren't quickly soaked in chemicals. Dreams were as slippery as trout, but she had a handle on this one, now. She even remembered the part about the lake. It was not Lake Hoopa, it was *Swan Lake*, a ballet her mother used to dance in, while Sissy, only eight or nine then, would watch from the corner the dancers performing certain movements with such grace that even recalling it made her want to dance.

She watched the girl with the inkblot — Liz or Lori? — take her card out and present herself for her routine on the uneven parallel bars. She was clearly on the point of panic. She rubbed her nose, scratched her leg, and finally saluted the judge. But then she took too long preparing for her mount, which was obviously a very difficult one. At last she attempted a straddle jump over the low bar, but her foot hung up on the bar and she sprawled! She clambered up and went back to the starting position. Again she attempted it, and again she fell. Finally she skipped it, and kipped up to the high bar. Then she remained there in support position far beyond the time permitted, as she tried to remember what came next.

"What's wrong with her?" Andrea asked Sissy.

"You'd look bad, too, if you'd never tried it before," Sissy giggled.

Bonnie squeezed her arm. "Did you see your score? You got an 8.3, even with a fall. — Oh, heavens, that poor Long girl! She just fell again!"

Just before the Butterflies moved on to the floor mat, Liz Long gave up and dropped out, weeping.

The Way It Works

The truth about Liz and Lori had come to her in the dream. All the facts had been there in her mind, scattered like bits of Indian pottery; but only in her dreams could she put them together. What had puzzled her was that when she herself had been a member of the Raskells, the Long girls had been very good gymnasts, but with weaknesses like anyone else. Lori was physically stronger than Liz, so she made a better showing on the parallel bars and the horse. But Liz had more grace, so that her big events were the floor and beam.

Sitting around the other girls awaiting their turns on the mat, Sissy felt sorry for what was happening to them. They had cheated, but probably it had been Ruby's idea.

When they called Sissy for the floor exercise, she carried her name card out to the tripod. Juno arrived at the same time and the official took both cards. Juno stared at Sissy with poison in her dark froglike eyes.

"My mother's going to protest to the head judge!" she hissed. "You upset Liz, and now she can't even compete."

"But it was just a little autographing accident, Juno! Not nearly as bad as Harry blinding me. Of *course* she can compete. We'll all be waiting to see her on the beam. . . ."

Juno thrust her face into Sissy's. "You're just a sawdusty carpenter's daughter, and we're going to tear down your hotel!"

Sissy's laugh trilled like a meadowlark's song as she trotted back. *Swan Lake* — how could she forget the year of *Swan Lake*? — when her mother could not go from one room to another without doing a stretch or a plié, an entrechat or an assemblé, while Sissy trailed around imitating her. The dance coach had shown Sissy some things and said she had real talent; but her mother had put a stop to it, snapping:

"I don't want her worrying about dance at nine."

Shortly after that her mother left to join the little ballet company in the South.

Bonnie bent over her as she prepared to do her floor ex. "Don't think about the moves," she said. "Just think about elegance. Turn yourself loose!"

A judge sat at each of the far corners behind a card table. A runner in a green leotard darted from one of them to the other, then carried the scores toward the raised judges' stand across the floor. The floor judges were watching Sissy as she moved to her starting position a few yards from a corner of the big blue mat. She gave the head judge a shy smile — just shy enough, for she did not want to overdo it. She felt so sure of herself that she was eager to hear the first notes of "Rhapsody in Blue." She raised her arm in a salute, then nodded at the young man at the record player. She was a small, straight figure in dark blue who was supposed to use that whole big mat as a piece of equipment.

As the music started, she executed her starting pose, then did some swingy jazz steps to the near corner. In her mind she saw a long diagonal line across the mat. She ran for her first pass, a roundoff; did a back handspring, then a full-twisting back layout.

Landing squarely, she finished with a lunge exactly in the opposite corner, her arms extended. *Swan Lake* with handsprings! She felt sure and happy, as quick and darting as the music.

A floor movement put her in position for a chain of back handsprings down the side toward the other judge. She moved down the blue mat like an electrified inchworm. She finished with a high stag jump to the side. She looked up at the judge, who appeared surprised and interested. Turning, she moved down the edge of the mat in a series of dive cartwheels, tinsicas, and back handspring step-outs. In the far corner, she posed and broke left toward the center of the mat, thinking out the next series of jumps and a pair of breathtaking aerial front walkovers. In the corner where the other girls were waiting their turns, she caught a glimpse of Andrea watching her with her hands pressed together and her face shining, looking like the little saint of the gymnasts.

My main fan! Sissy thought. The little saint with a cucumber in her purse. She danced to the corner in the saucy jazz steps Bonnie liked. And now she was in the final corner, and turning toward the heart of the mat.

She ran into a roundoff, a back handspring, and whipped over in layout position, her body arched slightly as her hands and fingers showed, in their elegance, that they, too, were part of the exercise. She leaped to a split on the mat, and popped up to the final pose.

The girls yelled. She ran off. Bonnie kissed her. She plopped down by Andrea, breathing hard. "So neat!" Andrea blurted.

"Thank you!" Sissy said. "How are the Long girls doing?"

Andrea's laugh burbled. "It's *pitiful!* Lori fell off the beam, and finally dropped out. So both of them are out of two events. They're only going with four gymnasts in Class I, now, They're wiped out! What do you suppose happened?"

"I *know* what happened. Lori's been doing all the bar and vault routines, and Liz has been doing the balance beam and the floor. But each girl's been doing the same routine *twice*, because nobody could tell them apart! But when I squirted ink on one of them, that ruined their act and they both have to do all the events! And they weren't ready!"

Holly went out to do her best thing, a perky floor routine suited to her personality. The

162

audience responded to her swingy steps and precise tumbling with applause. Holly worked all the harder, finished to the sound of clapping, and ran off. Patsy Moss followed her with a fast routine full of striking tumbling tricks. When Andrea's name was called, she jumped up and ran out with her card.

Cucumbers, orange slices, and exhaustive workouts had trimmed her down. She was lighter on her feet and quicker on her handsprings. Her poses looked spontaneous. She finished to a sound she had never heard before: applause from someone beside her parents.

The four teams moved around the floor. The girl named Debbie, of the Pirouettes, showed how flashy a vault could be. The Aerials went to the parallel bars. One of them left the high bar in a beautiful, soaring hecht dismount as Sissy watched. There was a patter of applause, and Sissy thought of the uniqueness of the sport of gymnastics. You spent hundreds of hours perfecting scores of moves — and who came to watch? Your family, a few parents of pudgy kids who thought the sport might slim them down, and fledgling gymnasts who wanted to study the right way of doing a routine.

Like most works of art, perfection was often its own reward.

The Butterflies went on to the vault, while Haskell's Raskells continued to struggle, dismayed and dazed.

The loudspeakers rattled. ". . . Sissy Benedict, for the Butterflies, 9.5 on the floor routine."

Juno scored 7.9 on her floor routine, and her mother went over and insulted a judge.

A few minutes later it was over. The clubs lined up for the news their coaches had already totaled up. In team scoring, it was Butterflies, Pirouettes, Aerials, and Raskells.

In individual scoring, Class I, Juniors, it was Sissy Benedict.

As they were changing, some small girls came into the exercise room. They picked out the club wearing dark blue leotards with colored butterflies around the neck, and went up to Bonnie. They said they went to school in Fortuna, and were taking up gymnastics. How good did you have to be to get into the Butterflies?

Bonnie told them that *getting* in was easy, but *staying* in was hard.

When You Want the Best

The small hotel might stand forever, Sissy thought. She could feel new life vibrating in its timbers as she, her father, and Bonnie sat at the table by the window. Her father had lighted a candle on the table by the street. No one present having a serious weight problem, Bonnie had approved the idea of ice cream — for this time only. Sissy still wore her leotard. Her father and Bonnie were doing a lot of serious talking with a pencil and paper and figures; something about more changes she wanted made to the gym.

But Sissy was reliving the evening.

I'm doing my handstand mount onto the beam. I think Ernie got a picture of it. I do an English handstand and a front walkover to a standing pose.

Nothing would ever dim the memory of tonight. She would preserve it in bits of blue yarn from her hair, in a framed score card, and in pages written in her diary.

"Are you with us?" her father asked her.

Sissy focused on his face. "What? Oh, I was thinking about something."

"Lots to think about," smiled her father, with an expression that was somehow not entirely happy. *He* was thinking, she knew, about thousand-dollar bills, lost forever, and about a Red Ball wrecker, waiting out there in the night with a bloodthirsty grin. For somewhere in Meadowdale, the Heinrichs were plotting revenge — savoring the first splintering explosion of the ball through the front wall of the Mark Twain Hotel. She was as anxious to settle that problem as he was.

"We were just talking about mirrors for the gym," Bonnie said. "I'm planning a half-wall of them, just like a ballet school."

"Neat! — Daddy, do you remember the day we measured the upstairs hall, to see whether the floor had sunk?"

"Sure. I thought it'd sagged, or they'd installed the baseboard too high."

"Well, I think it sagged," Sissy said. "I

166

dreamt about it the other night. I dreamt that wood gets tired, just like muscle."

"Fatigue, they call it. But shrinkage causes the same thing. I've ripped up so many old floors that I expect to find tons of dust and a few Indian-head pennies when I — wait a minute," he said, suddenly. "Are you trying to tell me something?"

"I'm trying to tell you my dream. I dreamt that it wasn't rats I heard in the wall, or a ghost moaning, but the wind blowing through it. The nest-building sound could be papers that have been sucked into it by drafts — "

"Now, I wonder — !"

Her father spilled his coffee getting up. He walked into the lobby and groped for something in one of his tool boxes. Following, Sissy and Bonnie saw him charging up the stairs, turning on lights as he went. They found him at the end of the hall with a small crowbar in his hand. On the wall hung a framed photograph of the hotel as it was before the turn of the century, when it was called the Hotel Denmark. He raised his head and sniffed.

"Steer manure," he said. "Mac Cameron fertilized his lawn yesterday and we'll be smelling it for a while. Smells percolate through these walls like smoke."

Sissy tore a corner off her program and dropped it on the floor. It lay motionless before the office door. "Now watch!" she said. She raised the hall window, and immediately drafts began to sigh and blow down the hall. The scrap of paper scuttled crablike along the dark, oiled flooring as it rode a draft. She closed the window, and it halted. "See?" she cried. But when she raised it again, it traveled on. She squealed. Inch by inch it moved, until finally it slipped beneath the baseboard and into the wall!

Sissy's father gave a yell and forced the edge of the crowbar between the baseboard and the wall. Prying carefully, he loosened the board and tossed it aside. Where it had been, a long dark opening about two inches high was revealed. Sissy dropped to her knees. Thinking about spiders, she groped underneath it. There was a fairly deep space where the flooring ended. She lay on her stomach and reached still deeper.

First she pulled out some wood shavings. Then it was an advertising leaflet for Rufkin's Wood and Coal Yard, and then a page of a letter. What if Mr. Twain had written it! But no — in his days the baseboard hadn't shrunk and the flooring hadn't sagged.

Then it was a half-page from a magazine, on which corsets were displayed. And a printed card with a frazzled string: PLEASE DO NOT DISTURB. And at last something with a tough, official feel — that special kind of paper! She grinned and pulled it out. It was a picture of a President.

"It really should be a picture of a gymnast," she said.

Her father seized it and kissed Grover Cleveland on the mouth. "This kid of mine!" he said to Bonnie. "She's going into all gifted classes next fall."

Next Sissy pulled out a floor-ex diagram, and a paper that said STYLE. (She knew what style was, now!) There was also a scrap of a dress pattern, a business card which said: ARLETA MORTUARY. WHEN YOU WANT THE BEST, and then another thousand-dollar bill. After that some more trash, and a final thousand-dollar bill. Her father took the bills and left Sissy with the mortician's card.

"When you want the best," he said. "Ladies, we've got the best. The best is right here at the Mark Twain. Watch for the grand opening!"

Sissy regarded the card with a misty smile, not thinking of funerals but of brightly colored leotards, springy wooden bars, and girls rising in high-twisting somersaults. She looked at her father and had to sniffle away a tear. She wanted the best, too, and she knew the best was yet to come.